MW01243340

THE RINK

Micheal Logan
AKA: Mikeylotheweirdo

VISUALWORDING

TODAY'S BOOKS ARE TOMORROW'S MOVIES

ISBN: 978-1-7370676-2-7 (Paperback)

Cover Art by Jeff "CoomCoom" Coomer

Editing and Layout by Ellen Gehring

To request permissions, contact the publisher at
Mikeylotheweirdo@gmail.com

Printed by Lulu.com in the USA.

Prelude

"Answer the door, Mike!" Dolores commanded her son.

"Yes ma'am" Mikey responded and quickly ran to the door. "Who is it?" Mike yelled, waiting for an answer before opening the door.

"It's Boone, dumbass." Mikey opened the door and gave Boone a stern look.

Dolores slowly walked down the stairs staring at Boone as if he was crazy. "Excuse me?" Dolores questioned with a surprised look, her tone, freezing Boone in his place.

"Oh, hey Ma D!" Boone said nervously, chuckling. Mikey laughed on the sidelines of the altercation between Boone and his mother. "Mmmhmm, c'mere you fool," Dolores spoke in a sarcastic tone pulling Boone in for a hug.

"Ight Boone, you ready to go?" Mikey asked as Dolores walked away. "And where y'all going?" Dolores asked, turning toward the boys.

"We was going to get the twins and then to the rink," Mikey answered.

Dolores nodded in agreement before she spoke. "Well go get dressed, you're not going anywhere dressed like that." Mikey nodded and both he and Boone headed to his room.

"So, I think I'm going to tell Lola I like her today," Mikey said getting dressed.

"Yeah, whatever nigga." Boone waved Mikey off, paying him no attention. "You've been saying that for over two years, dude." Boone playfully started pointing at Mikey.

"No, I'm serious this time B." Mikey pleaded.

"Listen, we all met when we was five. Nigga we are finna be teenagers in two years." Boone clapped as he spoke. "What do you mean you just now about to tell her. We all know you like her. Shit, she knows you like her."

Mikey stopped and looked Boone in the eye earnestly. "You think she likes me back?"

Boone's face said 'really' but he was speechless at Mikey's comment. "I'll see you downstairs." He said getting up.

Mikey laughed as he finished getting dressed.

"Bro, what do you have on?" Boone laughed loudly, as Mikey came back downstairs.

"What you mean?" Mikey questioned not thinking anything was wrong with his outfit.

"Nothing man, c'mon let's go. Lo and Lay are waiting for us." Mikey nodded as they started out.

"Hey baby, don't forget to call me every hour and be in by the streetlights," Dolores said, giving Boone and Mike a hug before they opened the door. "Hold up." Dolores went to the kitchen and came back out with a bag of Cheetos. "Here give these to Lo for me and tell them I said hey and I miss them." Dolores gave the boys another hug and sent them off.

Mikey and Boone went to the garage to grab Mikey's bike and skates. "Question?" Mikey said, breaking the silence between the two as they rode down the street.

"Wassup?" Boone responded.

"You ever thought about selling drugs?"

Boone's head tilted at the question. "What?" Boone stopped his bike trying to register the question Mikey asked.

"You know Gino? We could be better than him, hold up, take this left right here."

Boone followed Mikey as they went into an alleyway. "Where are we going?" He asked.

Mikey held his hand up, signaling him to stop. Turning around, he put his finger on his mouth, hushing Boone while they continued down the alley. Hearing voices in the distance Mikey slowed his pace to be as quiet as possible.

"Listen bruh. I'm tryna be nice, either you give me the pack back or you pay me." Says one of the voices.

Boone pulled Mikey to leave but Mikey pulled back, hushing Boone again not wanting to leave behind what he came for. Mikey looked around frantically, noticing a green power box. Mikey pulled Boone behind the power box as some people walked by the alley entrance where they came in from. Mikey watched as they stopped at their bikes. The two unknown people talked for a second before hopping on the bikes and riding off.

"Fuck, moms finna kill me," Mikey whispered in anger; Boone quickly hushed him.

"Who's there?" The voice blared in their direction. Mikey and Boone froze, hoping they didn't get noticed. "Yo! I can hear you, who's there?" He yelled again his tone was more violent than before.

"It's okay G, It's just us." Another voice said.

Mikey and Boone let out a sigh of relief and watched as two new people rode their bikes to what looked like their leader.

"You like the new ride G?"

Gino slowly turned his head at his henchmen. "What are you like 10? Nigga, go put them back. Fuck wrong with y'all?" He said angrily.

"But this one is for you." One of them showed off Mikey's bike.

"Yo! We have somebody tied up and you're talking about a fucking bike. Like we didn't drive up here!" Gino screamed pointing at the man who was tied up.

"Listen, Gino, you don't have to do this. I promise you I will have the money."

Gino shooed off his henchmen and bent down to the guy in the chair. "Listen, Duke, I like you and this is real unprofessional right now don't you think." Duke stayed silent. Gino quickly pulled out a gun and put it to Duke's chest.

"No, no, no, no, Gino you don't have to do this I swear!" Duke pleaded for his life. Boone and Mikey were paralyzed in fear.

"Look, I'm gonna close my eyes and spin around then shoot, if you live you will pay me." Gino spoke sternly leaning closer to Duke's face. "But…" he trailed off for a moment. "If you don't, hey?" Gino smacked his teeth while letting off a nonchalant shrug.

"Wait, I have a little brother, his name is Tei-" A gunshot rang through the air stopping Duke from speaking anymore.

Gino ran and his henchmen caught up as they fled the scene. Mikey ran out and picked up a brick of drugs from a stash spot he previously found and ran back to Boone who was still stuck.

"Yo, let's go! Snap out of it!" Mikey shook Boone, breaking him out of his thoughts. They ran back to the entrance of the alley noticing that the henchmen put the bikes back just like Gino said. They got on their bikes and pedaled as fast as they could to flee from the scene and hide the drugs. "Where we finna put this

Boone?" Mikey frantically questioned Boone who was still in shock. Boone's legs were pedaling, and he was steering but his mind was detached from his actions. All he could see was the vision of Duke getting killed right in front of his eyes.

They rode in silence back to Mikey's house and went to the garage. "So, we're just gonna ignore what we saw?" Boone nervously asked Mikey who was scurrying to find a hiding place.

"I mean we can't say anything about this to anyone B. We would be accomplices or something." Mikey replied, hiding the drugs under the floorboard.

"We gotta take this to the grave, Mikey," Boone said, calming down.

"To death," Mikey said looking earnestly into Boone's eyes.

"Literally." Boone gave a stern look to Mikey. "Too soon?" Boone let off a weak smile hoping to lighten the mood. "C'mon bruh, let's get the girls." Getting back on his bike. "Listen, I'm scared too but if anyone was to know that we was there we'll be next," Mikey assured him.

Boone nodded in agreement as they did their secret handshake before sneaking back out of the garage and heading to the twin's house.

Finally pulling up to Layla and Lola's house their small talk ended as a moving truck blocked their visions. Yelling from Tyrin and Shawna, the girl's parents, filled the air while they continued to argue with one another. "You dirty bitch, I knew you did it," Tyrin said, walking to the truck. "Lola, say goodbye to your mom."

Shawna started crying as she hugged Lola. "You're not going to take my baby from me."

"Yo." Tyrin noticed Boone and Mikey's confused faces as they walked up to him. "I'm sorry but I got to tell you something." Tyrin gave them both a fist bump before he continued. "Look, some adult things happened between the girl's mom and me. So y'all won't be seeing Lola for a while. You might want to go say goodbye." They both nodded and headed where Lola was.

"I'm just gonna leave you two be. Good luck champ." Boone said, walking away toward Layla.

"Hi," Mikey said nervously. "Hey," Lola responded. Mikey wanted to try to lighten the mood but couldn't due to the predicament they were in. "Listen, I always wanted to tell you this, but I've been so nervous." Mikey started to freeze up out of nervousness.

"The chips" Boone whispered as he hugged Layla. "Oh yeah, here I know these are your favorite." Mikey handed Lola the Cheetos Dolores gave him, making Lola blush. "Sooo, you leaving huh?" Mikey said with his hand behind his head trying to make small talk.

"Lola, let's go!" Tyrin yelled.

Lola kissed Mikey on the cheek and looked him in the eyes knowing what he was going to tell her. "Tell me what you have to say when we get older." As much as Lola wanted to hear Mikey confess, he liked her she didn't want to hear it yet. Mikey nodded as Lola stuck out her pinky. "Promise?" Lola asked.

Mikey shook it with no hesitation and watched sadly, as she said goodbye to everyone else and got in the truck.

Boone and Mikey followed behind the truck until they were no longer able to keep up with it. Mikey thought of going back for Layla but decided not to. The ride to the Rink was void. Mikey couldn't think of anything to say, leaving the silence to fill the atmosphere. They continued in their stillness as they entered into their destination. Mikey only spoke once they were ready to skate. "C'mon." He nodded before heading to the skating floor.

After a while, a small boy skated beside them until he introduced himself. "Hey, I'm Teivel but my friends call me T."

Chapter 1

The sun flashed over Boone's face forcing his eyes to open. A lavender scent breezed past his nose from whoever else was in the room. He looked around in a slight trance from the alcohol a night before noticing an unknown female in his bed, he questioned himself about what had all happened. "I went to a party, got drunk, came home with a female, but with who?" Boone went over the blurry details the night before, to himself. He tried to stay quiet and wait until she woke up, but his mind wouldn't let him rest. Boone slowly leaned over to sneak a peek at her face. "Please Lord don't let her be ugly." He prayed under his breath. "Fuck" Boone said as he caught a full glimpse of the woman that was in the bed with him.

Meanwhile, Mikey tossed and turned from the night terrors that clouded his thoughts. Forcing him to dissipate into a new world in his mind.

"C'mon let's go skating!" Gina said pulling Mikey's arm, he obliged and followed behind as Gina's speed began to pick up until he was no longer able to keep up. "You gotta keep up if you're gonna catch me!" She teased.

Mikey tried to pick up speed but was unable to move. His vision narrowed and the Rink began to shrink becoming this elongated hallway tracing behind Gina. Every stride forward was useless, only repelling him. Everyone disappeared from around them, as she turned to face Mikey with tears in her eyes. "Help me! He's gonna take me away from you!" Gina yelled in desperation.

"Gigi, take my hand! I won't let him take you away from me again." Mikey retorted, reaching his hand out to Gina. They both reached out to each other slowly closing the gap. A light behind Gina blinded Mikey from seeing the face of a black figure that hovered behind her.

He also reached for Gina grabbing onto her hair and wrapping it around his hand. "YOU TOOK EVERYTHING FROM ME!" The man screamed. Mikey thought it sounded familiar but couldn't discern who it belonged to from the demonic roar that came with it.

"Almost there, Gigi!" Mikey kept stretching until he could feel the warmth of her palm on his own. "BANG!" the man's sinister whisper echoed off the walls of Mikey's brain until it sounded like a gunshot.

As he closed his hand he woke up with his arm in the air as if he was reaching for something. "What the fuck?" Mikey kept his hand in the air for a little while thinking back on the dream. "I haven't had a dream like this in a while." He thought to himself wiping off the tears that unconsciously fell from his eyes. He picked up his phone and sent a message to Tia, who he's been dating for a couple of months. "Yeah, I think I'm about done with her," Mikey commented to himself as he typed out his message. "We gotta talk, give me a call whenever you wake up Tia." Mikey sat on the edge of the bed in turmoil about his dream, his heart started to pound through his chest at the thought of him meeting this dream girl in real life. "Yeah, I can't wait anymore, this ain't what I want." He called Tia and the phone was immediately answered. "Listen we gotta talk-" He was cut off by the constant sound of movement. "Yo!" He yelled, getting no response. Mikey was about to hang up, thinking Tia 'butt answered' until he heard Tia speak, but not to him.

"What do you mean, why am I here? We went to a party because Mikey couldn't make it, we got drunk, and you took me home."

Mikey tilted his head in confusion and continued to listen as the unknown male voice spoke up after Tia's. "Please tell me we didn't do anything?" Mikey could hear the fear in the question.

"I mean we did a lot; do I look like someone you could just sleep next to?" Mikey began to chuckle in anger as disappointment fielded his mind.

"Fuck!" The unknown man yelled again.

Mikey sat up at the recognition of the male voice. "Boone?" He questioned himself. "Ain't no way...." he was steaming with anger, as he took a closer listen to the conversation on the phone.

"Why you buggin?" Tia arrogantly questioned.

"Fuck you mean, why I'm bugging. YOU'RE MY BEST FRIEND GIRL NIGGA!"

Mikey sighed and disconnected the call shaking his head. "Welp, damn." He said to himself, still mentally unable to grasp the fact that his best friend slept with his girlfriend. "You at least could have waited bruh, come the FUCK ON!" He let a portion of his anger out on his phone, launching it as hard as he could to the couch across the room. He quickly got dressed, grabbed his keys, and headed to Tia's house. "I'm finna beat this nigga ass," Mikey said under his breath letting the anger take over his mind. He thought to just surprise them, so he used his spare key to get in. The house was quiet. Mikey smacked his teeth in frustration. "Know what? I'm getting all the shit I paid for out of this bitch." He soon made way for the kitchen, grabbing all the food he bought. Cereal, oatmeal, steak, tv dinners, etc. He didn't care if he paid for it all or not, he was taking it back. He went upstairs and messed up Tia's room grabbing all the gifts he bought and things of his own that he left before. Mikey made sure to stop by the bathroom and pee all over the toilet seat, also leaving it up, knowing it was going to make her upset. "Let's just be petty. I ain't got shit else to do." He hid every left shoe around the house in random areas then left with his belongings.

On his way home he saw T at a gas station. "This day can't get any better, can it?" He questioned himself as he pulled up to the gas station next to him. T was still in the store unaware of Mikey's actions. Pulling out $500 from the ATM and stuffing it in his pocket, he went back to his car trying his hardest not to fall from being dizzy. Mikey sat patiently watching like a hungry lion watching for its prey. "Yo T! Wassup?" Mikey shouted.

T stood nervously trying to play it off as if he wasn't. "Wassup G " He shouted back, standing his ground to Mikey already knowing what he was here for.

"Ew, what happened to your head?" Mikey said pointing to the gash that covered T's head.

T had been so dizzy and lightheaded this whole time he almost forgot he had it. "What do you want?" T ignorantly responded, already knowing the answer. "You know what I'm here for, bruh. You've been MIA since I slid you that three months ago. You're a real hard man to find." Mikey said as T got back in the car. T tried to unnoticeably hide the money in the glove compartment as he spoke. "I've been trying to get your money G, that's all." Mikey got out of his car and walked up to T. "Listen, just give me $500 bruh and we ain't gotta speak no more." Mikey said as nicely as possible squinting at the dilation and redness of T's eyes. It frightened Mikey a little bit but didn't detour him.

"After all we've been through you gonna let a measly $500 come between us." T tried to talk his way out of giving up the money, but Mikey let off an evil grin that sent chills down T's spine. This wasn't an ordinary creepy smile; it was something more violent and sinister.

Mikey was never known to be evil, but he had moments where you could see the darkness cloud his eyes. "This $500 came between our business, but you and I both know there was way more that came between us," Mikey said, peering into the soul of T who soon shadowed below him inferiorly.

"Listen, the death of momma De-"

Cutting him off. "Nigga if I ever hear you say my momma's name, I will kill you myself," Mikey said, still staring into his eyes.

T felt like he was staring death in the face and became frustrated by the hopeless state he was in. The nice Mikey everyone knew at this moment somehow became the ambassador of darkness himself. Mikey lifted his shirt and showed the gun he had tucked into his pants and nodded to the glove compartment. No words were needed in this interaction.

T knowing, he was on thin ice, angrily grabbed the money and handed it over. Mikey balled up his fist and lifted it as if he was about to hit T but he stopped himself. Within a blink of an eye, Mikey's goofy nice demeanor came back. He let off a smile and walked away. "Fuck!" T screamed in the car as he punched the steering wheel.

Mikey found an old receipt and wrote down a number before going back to the car T was in. "I don't know who did that but I'm glad one of your females finally put you in your place," Mikey said, walking up to the car pointing at T's wound. T's face screamed murder.

"What do you want now, I gave you everything you wanted." He said gritting his teeth.

"Well, I'm such a nice guy I thought damn, you ain't got no money so here's the number to my plug." Mikey tossed the paper to T. "I'm not gonna tell him how you are, and why our business is done. I'm not cruel enough to stop your paper. I once had respect for you cause you was like my brother and my momma loved you like you was her own but this will be the last thing I do for you." T stayed silent, Mikey understood and began to walk away.

T looked at the paper to see that the name of the plug was no other than Eli.

Chapter 2

I need some water,
Something came over me,
Way too hot to simmer down,
Might as well overheat

Lola cut off her phone alarm as she woke up. Checking her phone, she saw that she got paid. "Best feeling in the world." She happily whispered to herself sitting up as she did a big morning stretch. Lola noticed that she made $1,500 this week alone. She switched over to her social media just to pass the time. It was just turning morning. A new face popped up on her screen, "Mmm he looks familiar, but still. He does look good." She said to herself as she began to look through his Instagram page. As she scrolled on Instagram a message from Vel surprised her. Lola knew Vel never usually woke up this early unless he was working.

Yurr
Hey Vel
Good morning beautiful wyd
Bout to get up and hop in the shower
Well, I'm round the way handling sum things, once I get done I'ma come slide
Okay gimmie like half an hr
Bett see you soon

After Lola got out of the shower, she dressed in a baggy T with some boy shorts, planning to just enjoy the time with Vel. "Hold up, here I come," Lola yelled, hearing a knock on the door.

"Wassup beautiful" Vel said as the door opened.

Lola greeted him with a hug and a kiss. "C'mon." Lola nodded for Vel to come in.

Vel watched Lola walk in front of him admiring her curves lustfully. "Sheesh, hate to see you go but I love to watch you leave," Vel said laughing before smacking her butt.

Lola turned around, giving Vel a stern look.

Vel responded with a wink causing her to shake her head.

Vel and Lola made themselves comfortable on the couch, Lola cut on Netflix and Vel began to roll up. This was their usual… meet up, smoke, and have sex. But Lola pondered on the fact that after all, they've been through this is all they do. "Hey, Velly," Lola said.

"Wassup." Looking up as he was finishing the blunt, he was rolling.

"I was wondering..." Vel waited in silence so Lola could process her thoughts. "I was wondering if we could still chill without smoking?"

Vel looked at Lola confusingly. "You don't wanna smoke?" Vel questioned.

"Not only that, but all we do is smoke and fuck." Showing her displeasure.

Sitting up giving his full attention, "I thought that's what you liked to do?" Stated Vel.

"I'm not saying I don't, but we've been through a lot. Especially when my dad..."

"It's okay baby, you don't gotta say more. I just saw you was hurting, and I helped, and we just got cool after. I'm here baby. If you don't want to smoke and fuck you don't have to and you was never forced to. If you not down neither am I, but I'ma need this." Vel said while he lit the blunt and took a hit. He held onto Lola's waist as he smoked, making sure to blow the smoke away from her face.

"Thank you, Vel." She said cuddling tight into his arms.

"Anytime, but just not right now, I gotta use the bathroom. Get up off me." Vel said, chuckling. "Put something on for me." Vel got up and emptied his pockets on the table.

Lola noticed some pills in a bag fell on the table with all his things. "What's that?" She pointed.

"Oh them? Don't worry, that's not for me. When I get out of here I gotta make a quick stop."

Lola let off an unbelieving look.

"You trippin 'bout nothing shorty." Waving Lola off. He picked up the pills and pocketed them before heading to the bathroom.

Lola watched as he went to the bathroom and started to put something on until she heard Vel's phone start vibrating. She ignored the first couple of rings until she couldn't anymore thinking it might be important. "Vel, yo phone ringing." She got up and checked it as she made her way to the bathroom. She noticed all the messages came from a contact named 'Baby girl'. Lola's smile dropped, anger and confusion took over her mind. Lola was aware that Vel didn't come out of the bathroom. She went and sat back down pondering on what to say.

After a couple of minutes, Vel came out of the bathroom. "What's wrong Lo?" Noticing the attitude that covered Lola's face. She gave him a cold shoulder as he sat down beside her. Vel tried to close the awkward gap between them, but Lola scooted over more, not allowing Vel to touch her. Vel was confused while anger slowly played into his emotions. "Fuck wrong with you Lo?"

Not able to hide her rage from knowing she was being cheated on, Lola got up and pointed at the door. "You need to leave Vel." Lola held back her tears.

Vel questioned what was going on until he noticed his phone wasn't in the same way he placed it. "You went through my phone?" Questioning as he stood up.

"I didn't and it wouldn't matter if I did. I don't know who yo 'baby girl' is but she's waiting on you, and I'm waiting on you to get the fuck out my house."

Vel began to laugh menacingly as he sat back down, sparking the blunt up again.

"Vel, I'm not playing you need to leav-" Lola was cut off.

"Shut up bitch." Snapped Vel.

Lola froze in anger and confusion. Getting ready to start yelling; she realized the atmosphere changed in the room. Lola's body began to be eaten by goosebumps from the uncertain aura that suddenly capsulated the room.

Vel took a giant puff of the blunt before he spoke. "You know you've always been ungrateful right? After all that I did for you when your dad passed. A plus for me but…" He chuckled as he went on. "But for you, sheesh you were just so vulnerable. I couldn't help myself, a fine dame that was morning. Easy ass." He began to let out a sinister laugh without facing Lola while tears began to form in her eyes.

She sadly wondered why Vel would say anything like that. Lola frantically searched around for an explanation until she landed on the bag that the pills were in was empty in the bathroom trash can. "Did you…" Lola said putting the pieces together.

"There you go looking for shit again," Vel said calmly as he slowly moved his head toward Lola. Lola's breath shortened, noticing that Vel's pupils were so dilated they almost demonized his eyes. The red that covered the tiny bit of sclera burned with a blood red. Vel let out a smile as he got up, flicking the blunt. Waving his index finger at Lola in a crazed manner. He chuckled as his movement began to slow in the eyes of Lola. Every step sounded like a strike of lighting. "You know, you were so beautiful when you were so, desperate. You needed me… to make you into something. I made you into the bitch you are. WITHOUT ME YOU AIN'T SHIT!" He yelled, Lola was no longer frozen but paralyzed by fear and heartbreak. She wanted to move, to scream for help, anything but her body wouldn't let her. "Your worthless, you know that. Nothing but a nut to bust." Vel tilted his head and let his eyes wander, undressing Lola's body to his own discretion.

A tear of disgust fell from Lola's eyes.

"You… you…" Her voice was hoarse as she tried to speak but Vel put a finger on her lips shushing her as he was now in arm's length distance.

"A pretty good bust if you ask me, and I'm getting that whether you give it or not." Lola's heart skipped a beat at his words knowing what his intentions were. Vel licked his lips moving his face closer to Lola's. Lola was suffocated by her fear of reliving the past. Vel wrapped his arms around her, holding her in place.

"No...no..." Lola cried as Vel moaned, kissing his way down her neck. Lola's mind reminisced on the emotional scars caused by her father Tyrin. "GET THE FUCK OFF ME!" Lola shoved Vel with all her strength, it didn't do anything but break his grasp on her. Lola remembered she had a gun in her room and took the chance she had to run for it.

"Bitch, get over here." Vel gritted through his teeth from the pain of Lola kicking him in the groin before trying to run. Vel grabbed her hair, wrapping it around his hand as he pulled her back to him. "And where do you think you're going?" Vel whispered in Lola's ear while he rubbed her nipple with his free hand before forcing her onto the wall. He grinded himself on her backside as Lola's nose began to bleed from the impact. Her face was covered in blood and tears as she tried to break free. "Yeah, that's what I like, that desperateness. Show me you need me." Vel said holding her on the wall forcing his hand down Lola's shorts.

Lola screamed, feeling Vels' once soft warm hands now cold and hard traveling down the bare skin of her butt. "DON'T FUCKING TOUCH ME!" Wiggling and moving as much as she could trying to get away but Vel wrapped his hands in her oversized shirt. Feeling him forcing her shorts down under her thighs. "Please don't do this Vel. STOP!" Lola desperately pleaded.

Vel was no longer listening. He had tunnel vision fueled by a demon of pills and lust. Pulling down his pants revealing his member he moved closer to Lola allowing himself to trace the crack of her butt. Moaning at the softness, Vel pressed Lola harder against the wall forcing her to bend a little. Her legs were slightly off the ground, only held up by standing on her toes. With the last bit of strength she had left, Lola placed her foot on the wall and pushed back.

She fell back on top of Vel forcing him to fall and crash his head on the ground. She quickly got up pushing her hand on Vel's face and ran upstairs to her room pulling up her shorts as she went.

"Get over here you bitch!" Vel yelled following behind. Lola shut the door and locked it right before Vel was able to get in. With no hesitation, Vel immediately began kicking the door. Every bang sounded like a gunshot that cradled the door on its hinges, scaring Lola as she anxiously looked for the gun. The door banged open as she pointed it to Vel. "You can't pull the trigger…?"

Lola shot right by his head grazing the top of his ear, missing only because she was shaking. Vel shakenly rubbed his ear noticing he was injured. His face scrunched up angrily as Lola stood continuing to point the gun at Vel's head. "Get out Vel, I won't miss again," Lola stated, before calming her breaths.

Vel dashed toward Lola in ignorance trying to catch her off guard, she kicked him backstopping his movement. Lola quickly pistol whipped Vel making him fall back. He took a couple of steps back, catching his balance in front of the steps as he held his head from the impact. "You lousy ugly bitch, kill me, do it, pull the trigger."

Lola wiped off her tears deciding he would never see her cry again even though her nose still trailed with blood. She cocked the gun back and shot Vels chest where his heart was.

Vel laughed as he took the bullet still standing like it didn't faze him. Lola looked confused, not noticing any blood. She let off another shot and he let off a wince in pain but stood there. Still no sight of blood. "I always stay strapped up princess," Vel said, showing his vest through his shirt.

Lola ran and kicked him down the flight of stairs as if she were a spartan. She shot as Vel fell, but from her nervousness from the events that transpired, she missed the shots to Vels head. Vel hurried to the door as soon as he felt himself hit the ground. Chasing behind him she emptied the rest of her clip onto his car window as he drove off. Once she realized there were no more bullets in the clip, she let all her emotions pour down her face as she headed back inside the house. She slammed the door, locking it. Placing her back on the door she slid down crying. Lola held the gun to herself, staring down the hole of the barrel. "Why couldn't there be more bullets?" Lola depressingly laughed and cried until she fell unconscious.

Chapter 3

Mikey pulled into the driveway not knowing what to do, he was filled with so much rage and sadness. He looked in the rearview mirror seeing a pair of skates in his backseat. Mikey smiled and grabbed his skates knowing exactly what to do. He spun the wheels letting his mind scramble on the good times he had at the rink growing up. "Thanks, ma." He said, taking a deep breath remembering his mom was the reason he began skating in the first place. Mikey pulled out of his driveway deciding to head to the Rink, the only place he felt free from everything.

He pulled up to the Rink noticing there weren't too many people, a nostalgic breeze passed him as he walked into the building. "Haven't been here in a long time," Mikey spoke to himself while sitting and watching the others in the rink while he laced up. Finally moving onto the smooth floor, he began to glide. Letting his emotions take over, Mikey felt as if he was flying, soaring over all his own problems. As he flew to his own discretion, he felt some turbulence. His plane started to fly closer to his problems and he started to see his regrets. Watching his mom as she bleeds into his hands. The anger that he hid deep within began to disperse as he started to soar again, away from the ground letting go of the pain that haunted him in that brief moment.

"Hey, you okay?" An unknown woman spoke, breaking the flight that soared through Mikey's head.

"Huh, oh yeah I'm fine," Mikey said, blinking rapidly, wiping the tears away that traced his cheek.

"Doesn't seem like it to me."

Mikey stared into her eyes as he was trying to regroup himself. "You look vaguely familiar stranger." He said trailing off.

"I could say the same about you, but I'm usually in here every other week when I have too much on my mind." She retorted as they continued to glide side by side. "Bad flight?" She asked.

Chuckling before he spoke. "That easy to tell huh?" Mikey questioned.

"It always rains before the crash." The unknown woman didn't notice the sadness that clouded her face as she spoke. Once she caught on to the face, she was making sure she quickly masked herself with a smile.

"I guess we're just two plane crashes waiting to happen," Mikey said, noticing the shift in her movements.

"I guess so, I'm Layla," Layla introduced herself, letting out her hand for Mikey to shake.

"Mike- " Mikey stopped himself as they both finally realized where they knew each other from.

"Oh, my lord, Mikey how have you been?!" Layla screamed, hugging him.

"Well as you see we got a lot of catching up to do," Mikey said, hugging her back.

"No cap, let's go sit down. I think I'm done crashing with style for a while." Mikey nodded and followed as they rolled off the floor. "I haven't seen you in a while. I never thought you would come back here since Lola left." Layla said as they found an open seat.

"I used to pop in and out for a little while then I stopped for some years, till moms insisted that we come back like two years ago." Mikey trailed off hiding his regret.

"How is momma D anyway?" Layla asked joyfully.

"She not with us anymore…" The atmosphere grew cold and silent, the music that played was absent from their ears.

"I'm sorry. I didn't mean to-" Layla was cut off.

"Don't be. You didn't know." Mikey replied with a faint smile.

"So, I always wondered?" Layla questioned trying to break the awkward silence that flooded the air. Mikey looked up in confusion. "Why didn't y'all come back and get me. I mean I get it; everything had happened but still. I wanted to skate." Layla said laughing brightening up the mood only for a moment.

"You really wanna know?" Mikey replied, losing the small smile that once covered his face. Layla had a questioning look that told Mikey to keep going. He took a deep breath before he spoke. "So, the day Lola left, me and Boone found a pound of coke before we came to your house. We watched a man get shot because we had the coke that he lost. After we left your house, we ended up meeting his younger brother Teivel here. We didn't have it in us to tell him what happened to his older brother, so we kept it a secret. I didn't think we could have come back to get you without one of us saying something, so we didn't." Layla nodded in agreement as Mikey continued. "After a while me, Boone, and Teivel ended up becoming the 3 phantoms under-" Mikey was cut off.

"Deadman," Layla said.

Mikey nodded in agreement and continued. "With that, a lot came but we were good people and kept everybody straight. After like three years from getting our titles, we wanted out, Teivel's older brother Duke didn't die from the shooting, but Gino- I mean Deadman, ended up finishing the job. We slowly started to sell less and less and sent our customers to other people until we lost the title after Duke died. Even though he taught us what we knew, he never wanted us to stay in that business."

Layla listened without interrupting, honestly intrigued that he was the one she heard about growing up. "Wait before you go on, who is us?"

"Oh, Boone, me, and Tievel," Mikey responded looking away as she smiled at Boone's name. "Well around that time my mom wanted us to come here. You know she loved this place." Mikey looked around admiring the place he spent his childhood. "Like three weeks after Teivel's older brother Duke was killed, we suspected it was Deadman cleaning up loose ends. So, we told Teivel what happened, and with all that happening he just… just changed. I can't blame him, but he's been shady moving.

Once we finally made it here it's moms, me and them two, we had a good time but before we left T said he had some business to handle." Mikey clenched his teeth before he spoke, feeling the rage, anger, and sadness well up. Layla held his hand in comfort so he could finish the story. "I never let anyone keep their piece on them whenever we were out, especially around moms. She hated guns, so I was the one who would hold onto it and get yelled at. Well, T didn't have his cause he left it at home like he usually does because we were out with moms. He told me that he found out who the killer was. I trusted him so I gave him my pistol and told him to send me his location when he got there and wait and watch so me and Boone can come help after we take mom home. He left and I was waiting for the text, but it never came. We sat in the parking lot saying goodbye for like an hour. You know how niggas be." Mikey let out a small chuckle before his eyes darkened. "It was like time stopped; you would have never guessed it would happen. All I hear is Boone yell 'get moms out of here' and then no soon after just gunshots."

Layla covered her mouth as her eyes started tearing up.

Mikey took a deep breath to gather his thoughts before he spoke again. "I ran to cover her until the shots were done, but once I got there, I saw blood. I went to grab my gun, but I didn't have it, at the same time I got a buzz from my phone. It was Teivel's location and him saying that the killer wasn't there." Mikey stopped talking and fought back the tears that swelled in his eyes.

"It's okay," Layla assured.

"I know, I just felt so useless, it was my fault, if I would have said something or even just… listen to what moms was saying. I don't know. All I do know is that I could've had my mom here." Rage fumed from his face as he spoke.

"It's not your fault no matter how you look at it. It's not your fault." Layla said, getting up to hug him.

"But it is. The people around me always get hurt." His eyes grew cold as he took another deep breath. "Well, that's what happened to moms. I've been chillin since then but me and Boone kinda had a falling out not too long ago." Mikey said smiling, he stuffed all his emotions and masked it all with a genuine smile.

"Well, it's okay. Ever since I've known you guys, whenever you two fell out you ended up cool again," Layla said as Mikey shook his head in disagreement

"Not this time."

Layla's eyes opened wide knowing it had to have been something serious. "Damn Mikey, you just been going through it haven't you?" Layla said playfully.

Mikey laughed before he spoke. "Now you see why I was crashing."

Layla joined in on the laugh before she spoke. "So, I guess it's my turn huh?" Feeling comfort in Mikey's smile as she continued. "It's only fair. Well after Lola left, mom's kinda started drinking. Like drinking, drinking. She got abusive, and it got bad. Like I remember one day the neighbors heard me screaming and called the police. She was arrested and put into jail for a little while and I was sent to foster care because my dad wouldn't come get me. I guess something happened to him I don't know. Once she got out it got worse. She stopped drinking and moved to coke. I didn't notice until things started coming up missing and I was paying all the bills by 16. She was still abusive, but she got sinister. I didn't know what to do. And I had to keep the house up. So, one day I changed the locks while she was gone but she came in through the window. She opened the door for her guy friend, and I tried to kick them out, but they wouldn't leave. She started to cry saying she would leave in the morning. That she just needed a place to crash for that night." Layla tried to hold her tears back, but they began to fall anyway. "Throughout the night I heard them talking, then I heard her giving him head. Like c'mon have some decency or sum." Layla angrily added. "I ran downstairs with my bat and told them to get the fuck out but once they looked at me…" Layla trailed off, chills fluttered her body from the thought of the memory. They weren't human. Their eyes were black as if they had been in a horror movie. The little bits of white in their eyes were so bloodshot. I could notice the bags that hung under those dead eyes from a mile away. My mom said 'look, I know I can't pay you in full but take my daughter. Look at her she's young and beautiful. You like how I was, right? She'll only be better, ain't that right.' She completely ignored me like I wasn't there. I went to call the police, but the man grabbed my hair and pulled me down. He held me down and whispered in my ear 'I think I'll take your mom up on that offer.' I screamed for help, but my mom didn't listen while that man touched me. She only sat there just high like the fucking junkie she is."

Mikey moved closer and hugged her, comforting her the best he could now.

"Praise the Most High, I was still fully dressed so I had more time to keep fighting. I finally got one hand free once he got my pants off and I grabbed the bat and hit him. I only saw red and even after that I just kept hitting him. My mom tried to stop me, yelling at me like I was in the wrong. She ain't wanna say nothing the whole time and then has the audacity to fucking put her hands on me. Calling me a disappointment, saying she wished I was dead. That my dad didn't really love me. That she didn't love me, and she hoped I went to jail to rot and get raped." Layla let out a heart-filled sigh as she shook her head. "She was just so mean to me." Layla finished, holding in her emotions, but her face was filled with anger as she began to speak. "I hit her, not with my hands but with the bat. I saw blood and the neighbors came seeing me undressed with a bloody bat and what looked like two dead people underneath me. Of course, they called the police and said they heard screaming from me, and they thought I was playing until I didn't scream anymore. The police were able to tell they were still high, so the case went as-"

Mikey cut her off. "A teenager surviving an addict break-in and molestation." He squeezed her tightly while tears began to roll down her face. "I'm sorry you had to go through that Lay, you know you was always my best friend. I wish I was there. But I can say I'm glad you made it out alive."

Layla looked up. "I'm glad you weren't. You had your own problems Mikey." she took a deep breath and recuperated before she spoke. "I guess we both were ready to crash, huh?" Not giving Mikey a chance to respond. "Well, it feels so good to see you again. And I know you said you and Boone fell out, but do you know how he is?"

Mikey chuckled again. "Damn shit just keeps getting worse tonight, don't it?" They both chuckled before he continued. "Well, this morning I called my ex, and they were in the bed together."

Layla's eyes shot open in bewilderment. "Boone?" She exclaimed unsurely.

"Yes, Boone. It be your own people. I was literally calling to break up with her. All he had to do was wait another couple of hours. Like damn, horny bastard." They both laughed for a second. "How's my baby Lola doing?"

Layla's smile dropped at the question. "Damn, can we get some good news please it's not even past one yet bro." Mikey jokingly said.

"I know right? But some stuff happened with our dad and she's down here now. She's been down here for like a year, but she lives alone. She got a man, but they're done now after what happened today."

Mikey tilted his head in curiosity. "What happened today?" He asked, Layla, hesitated to answer. "As much as I want to tell you, it's not my story to tell." Mikey nodded, understanding the situation. Layla's phone rang, cutting their conversation short. "My bad Mike, it's important I gotta go." She said getting up while reading her text.

"Yeah, go ahead, it's cool. I gotta go too. But take my number. Hopefully next time we link it'll be happier things to talk about." Mikey said, giving Layla his number.

"Agreed, gimme a hug so I can leave."

He smiled and hugged her. "I missed you, sis."

Layla spoke as they let each other go. "I missed you too bro, I gotta go."

Mikey sat back down as she started to walk away. "Yo sis!" he yelled, stopping her in her tracks. "Tell my baby girl I said daddy's home." he playfully said.

Layla laughed, shook her head, and walked out of the Rink.

Mikey changed back into his regular shoes and headed out the Rink as well.

Chapter 4

"Hey dad, how you feeling?" Lola said walking into the kitchen.

"I'm doing alright," Tyrin said, coughing up blood into a rag.

"You're not okay dad! I'm taking you to the hospital right now!" Lola argued trying to help her dad up out of the chair.

"No, I'm okay! Let me go Lola!" he said, pushing her off him. He paused nervously hoping he didn't hurt her. "I'm sorry I just- I don't know what's wrong with me. Please just leave me alone Gina." he pleaded, stuttering while still coughing up blood.

"You called me Gina; you haven't called me that in years. You are not alright dad. Why won't you let me help you!" she contended. She wanted to help her dad for years, but he would never let her.

"I SAID I DON'T WANT YOUR HELP! YOU ARE SO USELESS YOU CAN'T HELP ME! LET ME DIE! I DON'T NEED YOU!" He hammered viciously.

Lola began to cry at the words from her father. They shot in her heart, tearing through the layers of flesh. She tried to deny it because of his sickness but the hurtful words echoed in her head. "Why would you even say that you don't speak that way to me." A liquor bottle shot by her head slightly skidding past her cheek.

"Damn I missed. Get me another beer, Gina."

Lola muddled, looking around noticing she was in the house she moved into when she was younger. "No, I have to be dreaming. This can't happen again. LET ME OUT OF HERE!" Lola began to yell, noticing that her pains and regrets are coming back to life.

"Don't make me ask again Gina, get me a beer. Even your useless woman of a mother was useful enough to get me a beer." Tyrin waved, sitting on the couch staring at the TV screen.

Lola heard a small demonic-like whisper coming from her father as he continued to sit on the couch. Nothing but static played on the TV, the sound of white noise and Tyrin's whispers shadowed over her. The living room grew bigger, and everything slowed down and time moved slower. "Dad?" She said tiptoeing to her dad fearfully. She hoped he wouldn't hear her come close.

The whispers grew louder and clearer to understand. "You are nothing, you are useless, you are a void, a lost cause." The whispers repeated themselves, encapsulating her from all directions and drowning out every other sound that Lola could hear.

She stood behind her dad shaking while tears poured out of her eyes. Slowly she reached to touch her dad's shoulder and the head of Vel dropped backward like his neck broke. Lola's eyes widened as she jumped back from the frightful scene. Vel smiled, sending chills down Lola's spine. "No, why am I here! Please leave me alone!" She screamed in disbelief. A sinister laugh turned into an earthquake that shook the walls. The unease in Lola's heart forced her to ball up. Lola felt like a child again, she was unable to do anything about what was going on.

"What's wrong Gina, do you not love your dad anymore," Vel whispered in her ear. He had the voice of her father; the stench of alcohol filled her nostrils. She continued to stay in a ball hoping that if she curdled up it would make this nightmare end. "Why do you ignore me, Gina?" Vel's body shifted into Tryin's but his voice remained.

Lola got up and tried to run, noticing that she couldn't wake up from this nightmare. Her first few steps were futile as her head was yanked back. "Let me go!" she winced in pain.

"Okay," Tryrin said, still having the voice of Vel. He threw Lola up to the wall violently grabbing her shirt, he pushed her chest into the wall forming an arch. "Now, let's try this again." Still whispering in her ear.

Lola's eyes shot open realizing she was back in her new house. The actions from Vel happened again but as she tried to put her feet on the wall to kick off, the wall became a soft carpet that was glued to her face. She no longer had a hand digging in her back but a palm that covered the back of her head. Lola tried to scream but nothing came out.

"Shhh, it's okay Gina. You love your daddy, right?" Tyrin said, slurring his drunk voice. "Good girl, this is why you were always daddy's favorite. Even over mommy."

Lola began to cry trying to fight her way out of this situation again. "No, I fucking hate you! LET ME GO!" She screeched.

Tyrin grabbed a bottle next to him and slammed it next to her face pressing her head into the carpet. He pulled out his member making Lola scream but once again not having any sound. "You were always a big girl Gina." Tyrin lustfully spoke, slurring his words as he evilly chuckled.

She squirmed, hoping to break free from her father's grip. "Please let me go, don't do this please." She cried out. Tears blinded her vision.

"Just stop fighting LOLA AND WAKE UP. WAKE UP LOLA!" Banging shook the area as she felt his member slowly slide closer to her areas. "LOLA WAKE UP! CAN YOU HEAR ME LOLA, PLEASE OPEN UP!" Tyrin began to say but his voice transformed into Heathers.

Lola's eyes quickly opened, she felt herself checking to see if she was still dreaming. Heather kept knocking on the door while Lola wiped her tears trying to get herself together.

"Finally, I've been bangin-" Heather was cut off by Lola hugging her. "I know Lo. It's okay, I'm here now." Lola heard another voice but through a phone. She looked up to see who it was. "It's Lay." She whispered; Lola was tired of crying, but the waterfalls kept pouring from her eyes. Heather held her comforting her for a minute before following her inside the house. They went into the kitchen, where they usually talk. "Before you say anything, Layla, I'm pouring us drinks," Heather said, putting Layla on speakerphone.

Lola let off a small smile, glad to be around her best friend and her sister.

"Now let's talk about what's going on," Layla said as Heather passed Lola a drink and some juice.

"It was Vel." Lola started.

"I'm sorry, I see we gonna need this," Heather said, bringing the whole bottle to the table.

"Is all you ever think of is drinking?" Lola jokes, making Layla chuckle

"I'm glad to see you smile again." Heather retorted playfully.

Lola took a deep breath before she spoke. "Vel came over earlier…" She began to tell Heather all that happened earlier including the dream.

Heather and Layla sympathetically listened to every word comforting her in small intervals. "Damn," is all Heather could say as she wiped tears off her face. "You know what you need, a night out." Heather tried to brighten the mood.

"I'm grieving, what makes you think I need a night out?" Lola jokingly replied.

"She don't need no damn night out Heather," Layla reassured Lola.

"Well, you haven't been out since you was with that dog ass nigga." Heather nudged Lola hoping to sway her answer.

"Last thing I need is another dog ass nigga Heather. I just want to sit home, eat ice cream, and watch anime." Lola playfully pleaded knowing that Heather wasn't going to stop trying to get her out of the house.

"C'mon Lola we can go get food and some new clothes; I know you can't resist shopping. Plus, you gotta get away from this house even if it's just for a little bit."

Lola gave Heather a mean glare knowing that she did want to get out of the house.

"Now I can agree on that, you do need to get out of that house, come over here for a few days," Layla said over the phone.

"Can I come too?" Heather excitedly asked.

"No, you got a home." Layla declined playfully, making them all laugh.

Heather looked at Lola with a smirk that was contagious enough to make her smile. "Yes, let's do this," Heather exclaimed.

"But first we got to clean this up, I don't want to come back with any trace of him here," Lola said getting up. Heather nodded to the request and headed to the living room. "Are you coming to help, Layla?" She asked into the phone.

Heather nodded to the request and headed into the living room.

"I'm at the Rink right now sis but I'm going to see you later. Call me when y'all are on the way to the mall."

"Okay, we should be done soon anyway ain't too much to do," Lola said hiding her disappointment, she wanted her sister here too, but she knew she was going to see her soon.

"Okay Lo, I love you."

"I love you too, Lay." Lola heard Layla admiring some guy over the phone before hanging up.

"Put your phone down lil girl and bring yo ass, Gina," Heather said jokingly until she realized Lola was frozen in fear at the name. The whispers of her father and Vel filled Lola's head. She became a statue silently tortured by her pains and trauma. "Hey, hey I'm sorry I didn't mean it. Maybe we shouldn't head out tonight."

Lola snapped out of her trance as Heather comforted her. She didn't notice the tear that began to roll down her cheek. "No it's okay, I think. I just can't be called that name anymore." she sniffled, wiping her face. "I think I need it. It could help me take my mind off of things."

Heather gave a questioning glance to Lola who replied with a faint smile. "Okay, you sure?" Lola nodded her head in agreement. "Okay, well just let me know whenever and I mean WHENEVER you ready to leave or if you change your mind."

"Okay, I will." They both began to clean up, Heather put on some music that led them into overdrive. Instead of just cleaning out Vel's things they tag-teamed the whole house. "This was well needed," Lola said, falling onto the couch admiring their team effort.

"Shoot you and me both," Heather said, turning off the music and sitting next to Lola. "You ready to get some food and clothes?" Swinging her keys around her fingers.

"What we eating?" Lola asked.

"You choose." Heather shrugged her shoulders as she spoke.

"Well let's just get some chick-fil-a at the mall, they got the best chocolate milkshakes."

"Dude, you have a problem," Heather said in a serious tone.

Lola laughed as she got up. "I got Lay coming too. I'm about to go get dressed, could you tell her we're about to head out so she can meet us." She asked before heading upstairs.

"Gotcha sis," Heather replied.

Chapter 5

After leaving the rink Mikey went to Subway to get something to eat and then to his house. "Ain't no way boy, ain't no way." He said in disbelief, seeing Boone's car in his front yard.

Boone saw Mikey eyeing him. He took a deep breath before getting out. "Let's do this," Boone said, fortifying his mind before getting out of the car.

"The fuck is you doing here?" Mikey said, getting out of his car.

Boone bit his lip in disappointment at his own actions before getting out.

"I just want you to listen to me bruh." Boone pleaded.

"Really nigga." Mikey said, smacking his teeth. "You remember what I said?" he said, hiding his rage. Mikey punched him in the gut. "I said I would never hit my family in the face." Watching Boone curl up covering his stomach. Mikey kicked Boone's side forcing him to roll away. "I know what you did. Shit, you know what you did. That's why you here, I respect the fact that you are owning up but why do it nigga?" Mikey said angrily.

Boone got up, catching his breath. "Nigga, you hit mad hard." Still gasping for air and clutching his stomach. "I can tell you didn't hit the liver." Boone finally caught his breath as Mikey shook his head in disappointment.

"You can't even take me seriously right now and you're the one who fucked up." Mikey spit in Boone's direction making sure it didn't hit him before turning toward his house.

"I am serious, I know what happened. I was there but you wasn't."

Mikey turned around facing Boone again. "Then tell me what I missed out on. Other than the fact you fucked my bitch bruh." Mikey said angrily, moving closer to Boone step by step.

"Well, I saw you was on the call, but you hung up before you could hear everything. But I had to get all my thoughts together because I didn't remember anything.

Mikey chuckled before he spoke. "You didn't remember anything huh?"

Boone clenched his jaw. "Just listen. I have never done this to you ever my nigga. Loyalty is in my blood, and you know this." Pointing at Mikey.

"No, I KNEW!" Mikey yelled, pushing Boone back.

"Listen bruh, I let you have those hits earlier because no matter what I shouldn't have done what I did under any circumstance but don't push it bruh," Boone said, smiling evilly.

"Or what nigga? You let me? Ight, how about this." Mikey said, wrapping his leg behind Boone's and shoving him to the ground.

Boone rolled backward, decreasing the impact damage as he got back up. "I'm trying not to fight back. You know how I get." Boone said, holding onto the thin string of calmness in his mind.

"I'm supposed to be afraid? Why do you think we was best friends?" Mikey said getting closer to Boone again.

"Back up bruh," Boone replied.

"Or what nigga? What am I missing about this whole entanglement you had Boone?" Mikey placed his forehead on Boones. They did this as a sign of respect whenever they wanted to fight, and the fight would never happen unless the other would push back.

"I'm not pushing back; I want to talk. You are my brother." Boone said, taking a step back.

"Well, I want to, wassup," Mikey said putting his head back on Boone's more forcefully just breaking skin. Blood slowly slid down the middle of Boone's head, traveling down the bridge of his nose. Boone's and Mikey's eyes never left contact.

Anger filled Boone's bones as if it transferred through the head contact. Blood dripped from his nose, and he swung at Mikey hitting his rib forcing him back.

"Bet," Mikey said, clapping his fist and palm together before getting into a fighting stance.

Boone bit his lip also getting into his own stance. "I see this is the only way you gonna listen." Boone threw a jab at Mikey's chest as Mikey jabbed at Boone's stomach. Boone's jab hit Mikey's face because he dipped down. "I didn't mean that." he apologized while stepping back.

Mikey smiled, snorting up the blood from his nose before he spat. Giving a nod before putting both his forearms together then putting them in the air.

Although Mikey was mad, he knew it was a reason why Boone did what he did, and he was going to forgive him, but he needed to let his anger out some way. They both fought a lot growing up just like this, but Mikey kept his respect for Boone because of all the things they went through. Boone let out a sigh as he did the same, placing his forearms where Mikey's was. This meant no more moving. They placed their feet in front of them, touching toes through their shoes. As they got back into their fighting stances, Mikey saw the sincerity in Boone's eyes making him only angrier at his confusion on how he could do such a thing. They both began swinging at each other's bodies going back and forth as they yelled. "Once you hung up you missed the rest of the conversion," Boone said, wincing at the rib shot he received as he spoke.

"What else did I need to hear?" Mikey said, jabbing at Boone's chest. Boone leaned to the side making Mikey miss and responded with a hook to Mikey's rib. "I have cameras around and one of my cameras caught the rest of the conversation." Mikey grabbed Boone's wrist as it flew to his chest. He twisted it outward and threw it away from him. Turning around, walking towards his door grabbing the Subway bag that he dropped.

Boone followed behind him. They were quiet until they went into the kitchen where they both sat, Mikey, pulled out his sub and a knife. Boone watched as Mikey cut the sub in half and gave one side to him. He pulled his phone out going to the video that caught the rest of the conversation and gave it to Mikey. They both ate as Mikey listened.

No, no, no, no, no

What's wrong? You acting like you're scared or something? I won't say nun if you don't

Listen bitch, I don't know what happened last night but I'm not finna just keep quiet about this to my brother.

Well, tell him I'm done with him then. I was getting tired of him anyway. He soft

You dirty, get out my house hoe.

Fuck me and kick me out? Damn, I knew you was that type of person

Why are you still here? Get your shit and get out.

Well, maybe you would change your mind after another good time in?

What you talking bout.... WHAT DID YOU DO TO ME LAST NIGHT BITCH?

"I got a little angry," Boone said, chuckling.

Mikey shook his head, still angry as he looked into Boone's eyes. He acknowledged this wasn't the time for jokes with a head nod as they listened in again.

Well, I threw it back if that's what you asking, not to mention the amazing hea-

DON'T FUCKINGN PLAY WITH ME!

A loud bang was heard through the speaker catching Mikey off guard. He looked questionably at Boone who was lost in the sub.

Rough just how I like it.

I will kill you if you don't tell me what happened.

You really have a gun to my face... you are a bitch just like yo pussy ass friend

JUST TELL ME.... What did you do?

...I spiked your drink

What?

I SPIKED YOUR DRINK! Okay, damn get that gun out my face

Get your shit and get out.

Mikey slid the phone toward Boone. "Listen bruh."

Boone waved Mikey off before he spoke. "It's ight bruh, I ain't worried about it. We fought it out, got it out. We straight." Boone put his hand out.

"Yeah, we straight dawg. Always." Mikey replied as they did their handshake and hugged. "I was going to break up with her that morning anyway." he playfully mushed Boone.

"So, all I had to do was wait one day?"

Mikey gave off an obvious look before he spoke. "Just one day my nigga. Like I wasn't really tripping about the female, it was all about the action." Mikey said walking toward his cabinet.

"I gotchu but there's a reason," Boone replied, grabbing the bottle from the counter opposite of Mikey. "But now that's out of the way." Boone poured both a shot. "Brothers for life."

"For life." They both said tapping the glasses before taking the shot. "How was she?" Mikey said, giving a sly smile.

"C'mon bruh…" Boone tried to hide a smirk as he spoke.

"She was fire won't she?" Mikey said still with his sly smirk. "Thick as fuck."

Mikey dropped his smile, surprising Boone whose face turned worried. C'mon bruh," Mikey said angrily.

"But… you right, my fault," Boone said, nodding his head understanding he was wrong.

"Her ass? Yeah, she was thick, but she gave some FYE ASS HEAD BOY!" Mikey said laughing.

Boone started to laugh with him as he poured another drink for the both of them. Boone and Mikey joked around and talked about everything for a couple of hours. Boone spoke on what happened at the party, telling the whole story while Mikey spoke about seeing Layla at the rink. "So, there is a party going on tonight, if you down. I mean we both ain't got no pull." Boone got up, reaching his hand out to help Mikey.

"I mean I'm probably not going to take one of these floozies' home but I'm down for a good time." Mikey took Boone's hand and got up.

"Now get dressed, we're going to the mall. I want a new outfit, also gimme some sweats and a tee. You know what, I'm borrowing an outfit because you messed mine up." Boone said following Mikey upstairs.

"Whatever dude, you know what not to touch," Mikey replied, waving off Boone.

"And that's exactly what I want."

He gave Boone a stern look making him laugh. "I'm just playing," Boone said.

Chapter 6

"Damn, you smell that?" Boone said, taking a big sniff of the air, finally stepping foot in the mall.

"We just got in here," Mikey said nonchalantly.

"And I just got done beating yo ass or did you forget that?" Mikey gave a mean glance over to Boone.

"I don't remember it like that." Mikey pushed Boone playfully as they walked.

"Damn, got beat so bad you thought you won. Sheesh, brother." Boone jokingly retorted. Mikey and Boone joked and laughed as they walked to the food court.

"You see them? Open your eyes fool and look at what I'm looking at." Boone snickered pointing at the three females in line at Chick-fil-A.

"Wait, is that…" Mikey mumbled to himself, squinting to recognize the females Boone was pointing at. "Is that who?"

"You know Shawty?" Boone pressured Mikey.

"I don't know, I had a dream earlier and it was some chick I didn't know but I think that's her," Mikey said unsurely.

Boone's head nodded in confusion. "Like a dream girl?" He asked.

Mikey waved him off walking to take a seat where he can go unnoticed while getting a glimpse of her face.

"Bruh, ain't no such thing…"

Mikey's mind drifted, after finally seeing the face of the mysterious woman.

"Or so I thought." Boone stared at Mikey, gazing off in the air pondering on his earlier dream. "What happened in the dream?" Boone questioned.

Mikey told Boone the dream, periodically taking a peek at the woman from his dream.

"That's wild, and you said that's her?" Boone was still trying to comprehend what Mikey was saying.

"Yeah, I'm sure," Mikey said getting up.

"Where you going?" Boone asked, grabbing his arm.

"To go see if it's her." Mikey noticed the two other females left her alone and headed to the bathroom. Butterflies fluttered in his stomach at the nervousness as he walked closer. She wasn't facing him; Mikey took a deep breath before tapping her shoulder.

"Excuse me, are you Gina?"

The woman turned around gracefully until she heard the name 'Gina.' "How do you know that name?" She hysterically asked. "Who even are you?"

Mikey cooed with his arms hoping to calm the lady down and figure out what was wrong. "I don't know where I heard it, but I got it from a dream." Seeing the woman's eyes freeze in terror, he continued to speak. "I'm sorry if I offended you, but it's important. Are you Gina?" He asked once more.

"STOP CALLING ME THAT!" She screamed, silencing all commotion in the mall. All eyes focused on the two.

"I'm sorry, I just want to talk." Mikey pleaded quietly.

"Well, I don't." The woman said as she angrily got up.

The other two friends rushed to see what was happening after hearing their friend scream. "Are you okay Lola?" One of them said.

"Lola?" Mikey retorted.

"Yes, Lay, I'm okay," Lola reassured her sister.

Layla gave a mean glance to Mikey until she realized it was him. "Mikey?" She questioned in amusement.

Lola's eyes widened as tears once again swelled but this time they started to fall. "Is it really you?" Lola questioned, hoping she could catch up on missed time.

"Gina… no Lola. Hi, I missed you." Mikey pulled Lola into a hug as Heather and Layla awed in the background.

Boone walked up seeing it was a perfect time, acknowledging the girls. "What about me? I want a dream girl romance." They all chuckled except for Layla who was fuming in anger. The audacity to walk up as nothing happened, the disrespect he did to his best friend pissed her off. Layla walked up to Boone looking him in the eyes furiously.

"Whoa my bad sis, did I say something rude or something?" Boone questioned.

Mikey mouthed 'That's Layla' to help Boone but he didn't realize.

Layla slapped Boone across the face, once again forcing all eyes of the mall on their table.

"I think I'm about tired of getting sucker punched today," Boone said laughingly before his face went dark. Rubbing the wound on his cheek. He hovered over Layla, covering her in his own shadow.

The anger that fueled him poured from his eyes seeping to the depths of Layla's soul. Layla's anger didn't allow her to back down as she stood giving a mincing look back. The atmosphere grew tense between the two, the mall was still in shock to see what would happen next. "Don't think I don't know what happened earlier, you dog."

Boone looked at Mikey with a dumbfounded face. "Yes, I told her literally right before we fought," Mikey said, looking away guiltily.

"Why you telling our business to a stranger?" Boone pointed at Layla, still not recognizing who she was.

"Nigga, that's Layla," Mikey shouted through his teeth.

Boone's eyes widened cheerfully as if a revelation was bestowed upon him. He went to hug Layla who quickly shoved him back. "Don't touch me. I don't know who you are." Her face screamed disgust and disappointment.

"Ouch Lay, why you gotta look at me like that? I remember when you looked at me with love and compassion." Boone said pleading as he tried taking her hands.

Layla slapped his hands off her own. "Don't touch me." She snapped angrily before Mikey got in between them.

"What happened Mikey?" Lola asked as Mikey laughed.

"Listen, Layla, it's okay we're over it now. I forgave him." Mikey said looking at Layla, her eyes widened in disgust again.

"I'm not you, I don't just be taking my best friend back after he slept with my girl." Lola and Heather gasped in shock, both let off a face of disapproval toward Boone.

"There is a reason and proof." Mikey pleaded playfully.

"Yeah, and proof." Boone jokes.

Mikey glared at Boone, shutting him up. "Listen just trust me, Lay. You still got the video, Boone?"

Boone nodded.

"Okay Lay, go with Boone he'll explain everything."

40

Layla looked questioningly into Mikey's eyes that begged 'trust me.' After a few seconds of silence, Layla gave in. "Okay, but even if it's a good reason I'm not just going to let you off the hook." Pointing at Boone.

"Understandable. Just give me a listen, Lay." He surrendered.

"Hold on, I'm coming with you." Heather intervened. Mikey and Boone both gave a sketchy look her way, almost forgetting that she was even there in the first place.

Lola notices the vibe and speaks up. "This is Heather, she's been our friend for a little while. Heather, this is Boone, and this is Mikey." Both Mikey and Boone waved.

"Oh, I know who you guys are, these two never shut up about you."

Lola and Layla blushed at Heather's comment.

"Oh, so you've been thinking bout me huh?" Boone teased Layla.

She ducked in embarrassment trying to hide her emotions. "It doesn't matter, I still want to know the truth."

"Well come on you two lemme show you the proof," Boone said, holding his hand out for Layla.

She pondered at his gesture briefly before accepting his hand.

"Ew, now I'm a third wheel." Heather teased.

"What about them?" Layla questioned, pointing at Mikey and Lola who was already cuddled up.

"Huh?" Mikey questioned, finally looking up from Lola.

"Nothing, gimme a call if you need anything, bruh." Boone chuckled.

"Wait, what's wrong?" Lola said, snapping out her turmoil.

"It's nothing, we'll let you two love birds be." Stated Boone.

Both Mikey and Lola smiled like children.

Boone gave Mikey a thumbs up and an obvious wink before he walked the girls away.

Chapter 7

"So how have you been?" Lola questioned Mikey as they walked, breaking the loving atmosphere of silence between them. It felt like a dream come true for the both of them, almost cathartic.

"You want the truth or…" Giving a pause, thinking about what all he's been through.

"I mean whatever you want to tell me." Lola postured her arms behind her as she fluttered her eyes.

Mikey let off a smile shaking his head. "Well, I only tell the people closest to me," Mikey said as he pulled Lola closer to him.

"Looks like I'm the closest to you." Lola snuggled in Mikey's embrace feeling a sense of safety for the first time in a long time.

"Well, we could always be closer." He whispered in Lola's ear.

Lola burst out in laughter at Mikey's words. "Slow down el Tigre, I just met you."

Mikey waved Lola off and began to walk again. "But you think I'm fire."

She side-eyed Mikey. "You aight… I guess."

Mikey clenched his chest as if he had heart pain. "That stung a little bit, you know." Joking at Lola who is childishly sticking her tongue out. The time they spent together was nostalgic, they felt like kids again. A new world where it was just the two of them, a place both would never want to leave. Their time together made them forget about everything that happened in their lives, earlier that day.

"That's cute," Lola said as Mikey picked up a shirt. "What's wrong with it?" Lola questioned, watching him make a disgusted face as he put the shirt back.

"You see, I'm tryna be handsome, not cute. I'm no child."

"I'm no child" Lola crossed her arms and mocked him, causing him to smile. They couldn't stay nor even be serious around each other.

"What's the occasion that's got y'all shopping today?" Mikey asked as he followed her into a shoe store.

"Oh yeah, we're going to a party tonight, wanna come?" Lola asked nicely.

"Mmmhmm a party?" Rubbing his chin and squinting his eyes as if he was thinking. "Sure, I can tell Boone I don't feel like going with him anymore because you asked me." Lola's eyes lit up at his agreement. His smile sent butterflies into Lola's stomach.

This moment they were spending together, reminded them of the times when they were younger. "You used to wear stuff like this." Lola teased. Holding up a colorful shirt.

Mikey smacked his teeth and grabbed the shirt. "I still wear these types of shirts, whatchu mean? This is hard." Mikey clowned, putting it back. "Sheesh, the glow-up was real." Mikey chuckled looking into the mirror.

"So, I have a question," Lola said as she walked in front of the mirror holding a shirt up to herself.

"Wassup Lo?" Mikey asked, hugging her from behind, placing his chin on her head.

"How did you hear about the name Gina?"

Mikey noticed the spike in her breathing as she said the name.

"I was wondering what that was about. But I really don't know. I had a dream, and it was you."

Lola looked intrigued as Mikey continued.

"You kept calling to me telling me to help you because he was going to get you."

Lola furrowed her eyebrows. "Who is he?"

Shrugging his shoulders. "I was hoping you would tell me." he noticed the despair in her eyes. Maybe I heard someone say it when we were younger and subconsciously remembered it. I don't really know.

"I don't know either." Lola lied trying to convince herself that he just made it up. "What else happened?" She questioned.

"We was at the Rink, so I guess I could have guessed it was you but you know we both grew up so I couldn't really tell who you were plus I was calling you 'Gigi' in the dream."

Lola clenched her jaw at the name, she hated that name to the core.

"You kept saying he was going to get you and you reached your hand out for me to grab your hand but..." Mikey sighed before he spoke again. "Before I could reach you, I heard a voice, it was a man's voice. It sounded very familiar, but I couldn't put my finger on it. He screamed 'you took everything from me.' and as I kept reaching for you right before I could grab your hand, I heard a gunshot and woke up."

Lola tilted her head and pondered on the dream she was told. "Yeah, I wouldn't think too much into that. It just sounds like a bunch of confusion."

I don't get it either." Mikey said, mentally brushing off the strange dream he had. "Now I have a strange question," Mikey said as they continued their journey through the stores.

"And what is that?" Lola batted her eyes again making Mikey chuckle.

"Wassup with that name?" He noticed her tense up. "I can tell something bad happened and I'm not asking for every detail... well not right now. Whenever you want to talk about it, I'm here but I just want to know what it means to you."

Lola took a deep breath before she spoke. "Well once I went with my dad, we watched a lot of Martin together. That was our favorite TV show before he started..." Lola bit her lip, cutting herself off before speaking again. "Drinking that is." Mikey grabbed her hand holding it to comfort her as she continued to speak. "I'm okay." Lola vaguely chuckled through the voice cracks.

Lola smiled at the feeling of true comfort and trust. "Well, me and my dad watched Martin a lot and I would do things that Gina did on the show to be funny, and my dad would always respond with 'damn Gina.' Just like the show. It was never anything wrong with the name until he started just..." She bit her lip not being able to speak and not wanting to cry in such a public area.

Mikey nodded knowing he shouldn't pry anymore about this subject. "Thank you, I won't call you that anymore Lo. I promise."

Lola waved Mikey off. "It's okay, don't worry about it too much. Like I said, It's not a bad name. It's just the history of the person who gave it to me."

"Understandable." quietness filled the air due to their thoughts. Mikey grabbed Lola's hand, hoping to relieve the awkwardness.

"So…" Breaking the silence. "What happened with you and Boone? I never got the full story. It seems like a funny story, and I need a laugh."

Mikey chuckled thinking about it. "Well, it's a funny one." He said. Mikey told Lola the story between him and Boone while they continued to walk through the mall.

They continued to enjoy their time together feeling as if they were the only two people in the world. They traveled through a couple more stores until eventually meeting up with Boone and Layla. "Where did Heather go?" Lola asked.

"She went home. She said she didn't want to go to the party and then winked. Some appointment she got or something like that." Layla shrugged.

"But she was the one who invited me. You know what? It don't matter." Lola dismissed her point, catching on to what Heather did. Lola knew she owed Heather one after this.

Layla began to show Lola the things she got as they wondered about. After a while, Mikey, Lola, Layla, and Boone all finished shopping, all getting new outfits for the party.

"Anyone know what time the party starts?" Mikey asked.

"They usually start at like 8:00 but everybody be showing up around 9:00." Responded Boone.

"Well, we got like 3 more hours till it's that time," Mikey said, looking at his watch. "I gotta go do something and then I'ma come pick you up, Boone."

"Yeah, like take a shower." Boone teased.

"You need one too B." Layla jokes, taking a sniff of Boone while fanning her nose.

"You gonna get in with me?" Boone teased closing the distance between the two of them.

"Yeah, you wish." Layla playfully pushed Boone away as they all laughed together.

"Well okay, sis lets go and we'll meet y'all later." Lola chimed in. Everyone nodded in agreement. Mikey pulled Lola into his arms as they embraced. She tried to pull back but was stopped by the glare he gave her. She was mesmerized, almost hypnotized. This was the closest they have ever been since they were younger. Mikey cuffed his thumb and finger under Lola's chin as they stared into each other's eyes. They both leaned in closer for a kiss, but she quickly moved her head and whispered in his ear. "Maybe next time, lover boy." Placing her finger on Mikey's puckered lips.

He smiled and licked his lips.

All Lola wanted at this moment was him as much as he did for her, but she didn't want to seem too easy.

"Bring yo ass nigga." Boone yanked Mikey away from Lola.

"We're gonna see them later on. Lay I'ma see you in a bit."

Layla blushed at his response. Both Mikey and Lola looked at both of them wondering what they missed. Mikey blew Lola a kiss before turning around.

"Ew nigga, you're an adult." Boone scolded.

Mikey smacked his teeth at Boone's response. "Always ruining something." He said playfully smacking the back of Boone's head.

"Aight nigga, touch me again and I'm gone beat yo ass." Directing his fist at Mikey.

"You don't want that work again boy." Mikey joked squaring up.

They were both in good moods finally being rekindled with their childhood friends. They both watched as Lola and Layla walked away giggling, telling each other about their conversations.

Chapter 8

Teivel walked into his house noticing his girlfriend on the couch.

"Hey baby, you're finally back," she asked, still not getting up from the couch.

"Yeah," Teivel muttered, stumbling into the bathroom. Teivel looked in the mirror at the gash on his head. "It prolly needs stitches but at least it's not brain-damaging," Teivel said, trying to make light of it. He winced at the pain holding onto his head, stumbling into the wall from the dizziness.

"Are you okay T?" His girlfriend questioned, knocking on the door.

"Yeah, I just tripped earlier," he responded quickly, hoping she wouldn't pry.

"Open the door, I want to see you." The door handle shook until he opened it.

She jumped at the sight of the blood that covered his face. "What happened, are you okay?" She screamed, making him wince in more pain.

"Too loud bae." He retorted.

"I'm sorry. What do you need? We need to go to the hos-"

"No, I'm okay. Just get me some Tylenol and the super glue." Tievel sat down trying to make the world stop spinning. He sat letting his thoughts take over. Whispers began to cycle through his head which left him in confusion. His voice began to scream in his head "IT'S HIS FAULT, IT'S ALL HIS FAULT." He tried to maintain a cool head as he struggled to get up. A pulsating pain fought against him as he tried to find his way to the sink in front of him. "Ahhh!" He screamed, his head rang, and shook by every creak, whisper, and even thought. "Babe, get me the Tylenol!" He could hear his girlfriend panting running around. Every step she took shook his brain.

"Here you go, baby." She said, handing him the medicine.

Teivel snatched them, swallowing all of them in one gulp. He felt them get stuck, so he bent down and drank from the sink. He sat down, feeling the relief of the medicine.

"You need to go to the hospital T." His girlfriend said.

"Nah, I'm okay. Lemme see that." Referring to the superglue in her hands. He cleaned the wound then glued it shut, squeezing it for a couple of seconds to keep it closed. "I'ma go lay down for a second."

His girlfriend nodded and helped him to the bed. "How did this even happen?" She questioned as he laid down.

"I was robbed this morning and when I was running, I tripped on some bullshit." Her eyes widened as he spoke. "I finally see how white people do it in movies…" He chuckled but quickly stopped from the giddiness he felt. It irritated him. "It was Mikey, I hate that nigga." Teivel got comfortable in bed before speaking again. "He caught me at the store, I left my heat in the car. I was running to my whip and tripped on the curb. That's when he came up and put his gun to my head and took all the money I had in my pockets. It's cool, I'ma catch that nigga slipping though." Teivel said angrily as he tried to ignore the pain.

"You better! I ain't get with no bitch."

Teivel side-eyed his girlfriend as she spoke. "Tia, what did you say?" He questioned her while sitting up.

"I mean you had it on you, and you didn't do anything, sounds like a bitch to me."

He chuckled in disbelief. "I sound like a bitch?" Teivel got up and walked to his drawer.

"That's what I'm saying, I mean hey I call it as I see it." She shrugged and pulled a blunt.

"Mmhmm call it as you see it, alright." Teivel pulled out his gun and pointed it at her head. "Call it as you see it right. I'ma bitch right." He said, cocking back the gun. Tia was paralyzed by fear. "Lemme ask you something, you ungrateful hoe. Where was your ass last night and this morning?"

"I don't know what you're talking about. I was at home baby. Then I came here but you weren't here." Tia stuttered as she spoke.

Teivel chuckled knowing she was lying.

"You're not yourself, baby. You're scaring me." She cried.

"STOP ALL THE FUCKING ACTING TIA!" Teivel yelled, swinging the gun at Tia's head, but stopped right before making contact. "I'm gonna ask you one more time Tia. Where were you last night? No, I'll do you one better. Who did you leave the party with last night?" Teivel got in her face as he spoke.

Tia could feel his breath breeze past her face. "I think you need some of your real medicine, not no pain pills." Tia tried to avoid the question.

"I just took it didn't I?" As he spoke, he noticed the voices in his head never went away, instead they became his thoughts.

"What did you give me Tia?" He questioned calmly. The atmosphere became sinister as Tia didn't say a word. Teivel looked into the mirror noticing his eyes were so dilated they seemed demonic. "Ahh, wrong pills babe." She said playfully.

"I'm sorry I was in a rush, and I knew you was going to need some later." Tia stuttered to get the truth out while Teivel motioned her to keep talking with his gun. "I grabbed the wrong ones. I was in a hurry." she quickly got up scurrying to the door.

Teivel ran to the door slamming it shut. "Where the fuck are you going? We're not done talking." He yanked Tia by her hair, throwing her to the ground. "Look at what you're making me do babe." He mocked going into his drawer where he keeps his medicine. "Eh I don't need this anyway, I always liked mine more." he threw the Tylenol bottle at Tia and grabbed his pills. "So now where were we?" He took another one. "Ahh. So, who did you leave with last night, Tia?"

Tia's fear turned into frustration and anger. "I left with Boone." Teivel nodded in agreement. "Yeah, you did." He walked to the door. "He was more of a man than you ever were." Teivel stopped in his tracks and faced her. Tia could have defecated on herself from the sheer fear that he gave her.

Teivel's wound opened a little, forcing blood to run down his head while his eyes were still pitch black while he smiled. "I bet you said that to Mikey for the last 3 months also huh? Getting the whole crew, I see you." Teivel said, still smiling.

Tia was stunned that he knew about her and Mikey. "I can explain." She pleaded.

"Yo cousin throwing another party on the Eastside, right?"

Tia kept silent thinking that he might do something crazy to her family.

"It's okay, you're meaningless to me and it was never your fault anyway," Teivel said, once again with a devilish grin. "Well get your things and be out by the time I get back or you'll end up like him."

"Whose him?" she questioned.

"Oh, you know..." He let out an evil laugh as he walked through the door. He stopped and turned side-eyeing Tia who was paralyzed from the fear that was placed in her soul. She saw death in his eyes. He was no longer Teivel, he was the devil. "It's all his fault, it's all his fault, my brother, my woman, my life. IT'S HIS FAULT!" Teivel's thoughts screamed in his mind before he finished speaking. "Mikey…"

Chapter 9

"I'm outside Auntie," Mikey said on the phone. "I came over right after I left the mall just like I promised."

"Hey, baby." His aunt Maya pulled him into a hug.

"Hey, auntie. How you doing today?" He replied.

"I'm alright, you know yo uncle in the kitchen like always."

Mikey nodded and went into the kitchen. "Wassup Unc?" Mikey said.

His uncle Will got up to hug him. "Wassup nephew. How you living mook?"

"I'm ight, just chilling." He noticed a sly smile on his uncle's face. "What's wrong?"

"Baby c'mere right quick." Will directed.

Maya walked into the kitchen and stood next to Will. "You see that twinkle in his eyes?" Will asked pointing at Mikey's eyes.

She stared for a second before questioning herself what it could be. She looked in awe at Mikey's face as soon as she realized what it was. "You glowing boy." Mikey looked confused by Maya's remark.

"You in love Lil nigga." Will teased.

"I don't know what you're talking about Unc," Mikey said breaking eye contact knowing that he was.

"Ooooh I'ma have some grandbabies- I mean." Maya stopped herself.

"It's okay Auntie, y'all been like a mom and dad to me growing up even before my moms passed."

It became cold and silent for a moment while everyone collected their thoughts. "C'mere boy." Will grabbed Mikey's hand and pulled him into a hug. Maya hugged Mikey from the side and Will covered them both.

"But y'all remember the twins?" Mikey questioned breaking away.

Maya and Will looked at each other not knowing what Mikey was talking about.

"From way back in the day? Layla and Lola."

Will's eyes widened at the remembrance. "They were really pretty. The ones from the rink, right?"

He nodded at Will's revelation.

"I liked them, how are they doing?" Not allowing Mikey to answer, he spoke again. "Wait, I thought they both moved with their dad," Will said.

Maya shook her head in disagreement. "No, remember what happened to their mom?" She tried to whisper low enough that Mikey couldn't hear.

"What happened?" Mikey asked, forgetting what Layla told him earlier.

"You don't know?" she sadly questioned.

"Oh wait, never mind. I think I know what you're talking about auntie" recollecting the story he was told. He let his imagination take over as the thought of the scene played in its way in his brain.

"Mikey?" Maya called breaking him out of his daydream.

"Yeah, I see you definitely gotta know. Shit like that… Damn," Will said with a weak chuckle.

"Oh lord. I gotta get that." Maya rushed out of the kitchen to get her phone.

"So, it was..." Will paused in confusion of which twin Mikey liked. "I'm probably about to mix them up.

"Lola Unc." Mikey chimed in.

"I knew that nigga." he joked. "What? Y'all met up or something?" He questioned as he went to make a drink.

"Uhhh, we did today actually. Funny story is I had a dream about her earlier with a different name that her father only called her once she moved."

Will turned around in confusion at his remark. "What?" Mikey elaborated on the crazy dream he had earlier. "Hmmm, that's a weird one." His uncle said, taking a drink from his cup.

"Yeah, I know right, I don't know who that guy was, but his voice was just so familiar." Mikey got up to pour himself a drink.

"Pour me another one while I go grab something real quick." Mikey gave a puzzling look into Will's cup seeing he drank it all through the dream story. "Unc? You drink all that, that fast?" He said surprised.

"Nigga, just make me a drink." Will laughed as he left the kitchen.

"Gotcha Unc."

Will made his way to the basement, he felt around the wall knocking until he heard a hollowness. Will removed the brick that revealed a secret compartment. He looked around to make sure no one was watching and grabbed a chrome nine-millimeter pistol with a pearl handle, gold trimmings, a silencer, and an inscription that said 'no remorse' on the side of the barrel.

"What you doing down there bae," Maya yelled to him.

"Nun, just grabbing something for Mikey." He responded making his way back to the kitchen hiding the pistol from her view. He nodded for Mikey to come close.

"Yessir?" Mikey whispered.

"Run me to the store right quick, I gotta show you something."

Mikey nodded and made his way to the door.

"You're leaving already baby?" Maya asked.

"No ma'am, I'm taking Unc to the store right quick. You need anything auntie?"

She nodded and gave them both a hug. "Grab me some milds and a sprite."

"We got you baby." Will leaned in and kissed her. "Love you. See you in a bit." He said, closing the door behind him. "I'm driving." Will gestured his head to his truck. He recently got new speakers in it and wanted to show Mikey how they sounded. "Yeah, I just got these put in, that's what I called you over for. My bad, I just wanted you to hear them." Mikey waved off his apology. They both bobbed their heads to the beat and headed to the store. The music blared through the speakers vigorously vibrating the truck and shaking the neighborhood they drove through.

Mikey smiled watching his uncle enjoy his time in the thick bass dancing while he drove to the store and back.

When they finally pulled up to the house Will hesitated to get out. "That was the main reason I called you over, but this is what I have to give you now." he reached into his shirt pulling out the golden pistol he grabbed from the basement.

Mikey stared in amazement at the beauty of the gun before giving a doubtful look at Will. "I can't take this; grandpa gave it to you." Mikey pushed the gun away.

"Just take it. All your cousins in jail except Lil Mike and we both know this is not what he needs in his life path."

Mikey got quiet, pondering on Lil Mike. He was a gospel musician. Not big but did a bunch of shows around the country.

"Here, I want you to have it. I know you have one but this one is special. I don't know why but it protects the owner in dire situations, it saved my life a couple of times too. I almost wanna take back," Will jokingly said.

Mikey chuckled as he took the gun. He fiddled with it, getting comfortable with the weight and feeling. It was a lot heavier than the pistol he already had. "Nah Unc, this is dope," Mikey stated, still dazed at its beauty.

His uncle chuckled before he spoke. "Now it wouldn't be special if it was just a colorful regular degular ass pistol, would it? This pistol was made by your great grandfather, he made an exact replica of the gun in 'The Octopus Arm.' He loved this gun, he passed it down to your grandpa and he gave it to me. Now, I'm giving it to you." Mikey was in a daze at the story behind the pistol. He always saw the book 'The Octopus Arm' but he never got the gist nor read it.

"I gotta read that soon." He thought to himself.

"Now with this dream you had, I don't know what's coming, but I'm praying for your safety, stay alert Lil man I don't need to lose anyone else, okay?"

Mikey nodded, hugging him. "Yessir."

"I've always asked myself." Will was put into a daze from his thoughts. "How much could happen in a day. I've learned that you would be surprised about how much you could gain in a moment but also how much you could lose in an instant. Protect what's yours mook." Mikey accepted Will's words of wisdom. "Thanks again Unc."

"No problem, now come on before your aunt starts thinking sums up." They both laughed as they got out and headed into the house.

Mikey tucked the gun out of Maya's view before walking in behind Will. They all headed into the kitchen and sat down.

Maya poured everyone a drink. "To family, prosperity, and the grace of God," she said before turning on music.

They all toasted and took a shot. Mikey smiled at his aunt and uncle's playful banter that came shortly after. This was home for him even before his mother's murder and especially after.

"What you got planned for tonight?" Will questioned.

"I gotta party to go too," Mikey responded, taking another sip from his cup. They all had a high tolerance to alcohol, so the drink didn't impair them too much to be noticed.

"Better be careful, a party ain't a party until a fight breaks out." Maya chimed in, earning a laugh. "What time you heading out?" She asked. He bit his lip with regret.

"Right now, dude? For real?" Will said with a bit of disappointment. Mikey knew they wanted to spend time with him, but he couldn't back out of this chance to rekindle with Lola again.

"I'll be here again tomorrow I promise, and I'll bring Lola with me." He assured, hoping they wouldn't be too upset.

"There's that cheeky lover boy smile. Gone get out of here mook." Will chucked getting up to hug him. Mikey hugged them both before heading out.

"Love y'all!" He yelled, waiting for a response.

"Love you too baby" "Love you too mook." His aunt and uncle responded before he shut the door.

Mikey sat in the car marveling at the gun one more time before hiding it under his seat next to his other one. He sent a message to Boone telling him he was on his way home to change and then to come pick him up.

Chapter 10

"Yeah, c'mon I'm out here," Mikey said over the phone to Boone.

"Bet, I'm on my way out," Boone replied.

"And hurry up too. We already late as is."

Boone smacked his teeth before he spoke. "Bruh I'm black. Ain't no such thing as late. You know we move on colored people time" Boone joked before hanging up the phone.

Mikey let out a chuckling sigh while shaking his head. He put his phone back in his pocket. Five minutes passed before Boone walked out of the house and got into the car. "Nigga?!" Mikey questioned irritatingly.

"What?" Boone exclaimed with a small chuckle. "I told you I was black right?"

Mikey paid him no mind and started up the car. Mikey told Boone about what happened at his uncle's house as they headed to the party.

"Wait, you didn't tell him, right?" Boone fearfully questioned not wanting to let them down. Even though he had a family they moved away leaving him with Mikey and his mom. Mikey's uncle was like a father to both of them throughout all their life.

"Of course, I didn't tell him bruh." Mikey gave him a dumb look before Boone let out a sigh of relief. "I'm not that petty, plus we already handled the situation."

Boone nodded in agreement. "Well, hurry up and park this piece of shit so I can see this 'golden gatt' you talm bout nigga." He playfully remarked.

After finding a spot, Mikey reached under the seat grabbing the gun his uncle gave him. "It's chrome, not golden. Dummy." Mikey handed it over.

"Yeah, aight." Boone sat turning and twisting the gun in awe of its beauty.

"That hoe nice ain't it?" Mikey reached over grabbing the gun from Boone.

"Hell yeah, that bitch pretty. I really like that 'no remorse' on it, though. Adds a nice touch." Boone pointed at the inscription.

Mikey smirked, nodding in agreement gently rubbing his fingers across the writing.

"Them the girls right there," Boone said, breaking Mikey out of his thoughts and awe of the gun. Looking out for Lola and Layla, he tucked the gun in his pants, not wanting to see he had one on him.

Lola waived as she parked next to Mikey. Layla quickly got out of the passenger seat smiling ear to ear as she ran to hug Boone.

Mikey looked over to Boone, but he was already out of the car holding Layla in his arms kissing all over her face. "What happened between them?" He asked himself about their closeness. He got out of his car and sat in the empty passenger seat of Lola's car while she checked her lashes in the mirror, not paying any attention.

"Hey Layla, can you hand me my lash curler out of my purse." She said not knowing that Mikey sat in the car.

"Wrong person Lo."

She jumped at his voice. "Don't do that, you scared me half to death." Screaming playfully in relief. She was excited to see him again but didn't want to seem overly excited in his eyes, she decided to play it nonchalantly and get back to her lashes. "Well, it doesn't matter. Mike hand me that out my purse." She held her hand out waiting for Mikey to give her what she asked for.

"Yeah, yeah, yeah." He muttered under his breath handing her what she wanted.

"Thank you very much, handsome."

Mikey's eyes widened at her remark. "Oooooh you said I was handsome." He teases.

She quickly finished her lashes as Mikey sat with a cheeky smirk staring. "Yup and?" she closed her mirror and stared directly into his eyes.

"I hope there's more where that came from. That's all I'm saying" he said seductively, slowly moving closer to her face.

"Lemme think about that." she tapped her chin as she looked away playfully. "Hmmm, only if you're lucky." She said looking back at Mikey.

"And what's your meaning of lucky?" he asked, moving closer again. Lola leaned in closing the distance between them, as they were locked into each other's gaze desirably. She slowly leaned in as if she was going to kiss him. "Well, I guess you'll just have to find out huh?" She said stopping right before their lips could touch.

Mikey smacked his teeth, opening his eyes fully. "You be playing too much, one day I'm not gone listen and I'ma just kiss you while you talking." They laughed but Lola wanted nothing more than that.

"C'mon, we late!" Boone yelled banging on the window, breaking their moment.

"You better stop banging on my damn window Boone!" Lola shouted back making everyone laugh as they got out.

"I thought you said we black ain't no such thing as late." Mikey cheekily replied forcing Boone to smack his teeth.

"Don't matter nigga, bring yo ass" Mikey remembered that he still had the pistol tucked in his pants. "Shit" he whispered to himself. "Wassup?" Boone asked. Mikey waved him off nonchalantly, not wanting him to worry.

He looked around for a second before tucking it under the seat he was in. He got out jogging to catch up to them. As they got close to the entrance, he prayed he wouldn't see Tia at this party knowing the host is her cousin.

"Y'all ready?" Boone said joyfully as they lined up in front of the bodyguard. "Wassup Metri, still bodyguarding I see," Boone said while he got patted down.

"Pays more than just free ass," Metri replied jokingly. Boone and Mikey laughed but the girls didn't, feeling disgusted knowing females would really do it just to get into one of these parties.

"I'm sorry, I didn't know y'all was with them. I usually keep my manners in front of beautiful women." Metri apologized, pulling out his metal detector wand. "Any weapons, tasers, pocketknives, or knuckles?" Metri asked, waving the wand around them.

"Knuckles?" Layla asked jokingly.

"Hey, you never know." Metri shrugged as they chuckled.

"You're right, but no we don't."

Metri told them to wait while he grabbed some wristbands and pepper spray for the girls. "All y'all gimmie y'all hands. Everyone got a wristband on, and Metri handed Lola and Layla their own pepper spray. "It's not lethal but it is dangerous, so it'll give you enough time to contact me or one of the two dumbasses you came with." Metri pointed at Mikey and Boone who were making dumb faces behind the girls. They laughed at the two. Metri shook his head, taking a step to the side, allowing them to walk into the house.

The music blared as they opened the door. Seeing people dancing everywhere while the light strobed in patterns rotating around. They found a clear path to the kitchen and took it squeezing past people. Mikey grabbed the first bottle he saw that was not open. "Looks like we're keeping it holy tonight." He joked showing them the Christian Brothers bottle. They all gave a disappointed nod at the joke. "What? You want some New Testament Paul instead?"

"Please just- just stop." Boone slammed his palm on his head causing everyone to laugh. "Gimmie that bottle," Boone said, grabbing the Christian Brothers from Mikey. "Go get some shot glasses."

Mike mugged Boone before he spoke. "No sir, I'm getting Lola, Layla, and I shot glasses. Since you wanna run shit. Run yo ass over and get yo own… Nigga." Mikey said playfully, emphasizing his last word.

Boone chuckled and looked at Layla. "I gotchu babe, we don't wanna hang with these scrubs anyway." Boone put his arm around Layla's shoulders pulling her closer to him.

"Wait, what?" Layla was surprised, being broken from her conversation with her sister.

"Here take her too, we don't want her punk ass either." Boone playfully pushed Lola in Mikey's arms while they laughed.

"We ain't wanna hang with yo sucka set no way buster." Mikey imitated a California gangster while catching and holding onto Lola. Boone winked and soon disappeared from Mikey's field of vision leaving him and Lola. He nodded in respect knowing they will meet up once it was time to go.

"Well, how do I always end up here?" Lola teased looking at Mikey. She never stopped looking at him since she was pushed, she just admired his looks. He smiled back looking down at her. The spotlight glistened off her honey brown eyes that sank Mikey into them. They stood still as the world slowed down around them, silently drowned in each other's gaze.

"Well, you wanna take a shot or you just gone keep drooling over me, baby girl?" Mikey teased.

Chapter 11

"Oh, so I'm baby girl now?" Lola questioned trying to hide her blushing at the pet name she received.

"Only if you act right." Mikey joked, pouring shots. "I'ma keep it a bean with you baby girl, I kinda can't drink liquor straight."

"Well then, someone has to drive home anyway, I'll have what you're having." she nodded to his cup. He smiled at her response. "What are you smiling for?" seeing his childlike smile, she never really saw him smile too much from the time they spent together. His laugh she heard, but a smile like this she has never seen, made her heart flutter.

"I'm just happy to have you around again Lo, I really missed you." He said, handing her a drink. "To our reunion." He lifted his cup to make a toast.

"To us," she corrected.

He was bewildered at her remark. He tapped her cup not hiding his happiness anymore, they both were ecstatic to be in each other's presence once again. Once they finished their first cup Mikey began filling up the next cup before heading to the backyard. "C'mon baby girl, let's find a spot to sit." He grabbed her hand and scanned the open yard finding an empty table, not near anyone.

"This is a really big house." She admired the size as they traveled through the crowd to the table.

"Yeah, Heem been throwing these shindigs ever since he got this big ass house."

Lola spits up her drink in laughter at his choice of words. "Shindig?" She said through her laughter.

Mikey gave a stern look that only made Lola laugh harder. "Whatever nigga." Mikey smacked his teeth, waving her off as they continued to walk.

"Okay, who's Heem or whatnot." She asked, finally recuperating from her laughter.

"He's been doing this for a while, like once or twice every month. But he's one of my old friends' cousins from back in the day." He watched the random people partying at the poolside, hoping she didn't pry on who this old friend was. The music blared outside the house, everyone was having a good time, Mikey and Lola watched in amusement. "Yeah, Nah they wilding." he said watching some men make a sign that said, 'No tops in the pool.'

She noticed and shook her head in disapproval. They watched as the men walked around the pool with a megaphone telling all the females in the pool no tops were allowed. All the women looked at each other and shrugged, taking off their bikini bras and shirts. A domino effect happened after two females took theirs off causing the crowd to cheer.

Mikey looked in amusement at the fact that it was that simple for females to be half-naked. "Yeah, this is not my type of place." taking a sip from his drink.

"It looks like it might be." Lola slyly remarked.

He responded with a face that just said 'really.' "There are tiddies everywhere and you expect me not to look?" He playfully questioned.

Lola shrugged, taking a sip from her cup.

"Hypocrite," Mikey said fake coughing.

She smacked her teeth before she spoke. "Those are some big thongs though."

He burst into laughter at her remark. His phone soon started to buzz. It was Boone. "Yeah, wassup?"

"You see those tiddies nigga?" Boone yelled playfully; a slap was heard quickly after.

"Nigga, where are you?" Mikey said laughing.

"Look up dummy." Boone waved as Mikey finally saw him. They were on the balcony on the third floor. Boone has been coming to these parties forever; he always gets special passes to third-floor rooms.

Mikey pointed him out to Lola while she saw her sister. They both waved at each other, Layla pointed at the lady with the biggest breasts and made a curve around her breasts imitating the other woman's. Lola chuckled acknowledging who her sister was talking about.

"Well, I'm finna do what it do dawg, talk to you in an hour," Boone smirked menacingly.

"More like five minutes." Mikey joked back.

"Don't hate me cause I'm beautiful dawg. Maybe if you fix that yee yee ass haircut of yours, Lola might get on yah dick." Boone quickly hung up and flicked Mikey off.

Layla slapped Boone again hearing what he said. Boone called back as Mikey flicked him back off. "Nigga." Boone sang, imitating Lamar from the Grand Theft Auto game. They went back into the room, closing the curtains after waving bye.

Mikey looked back at Lola while they both laughed at Boone and Layla. "I love them together man." Mikey smiled. Lola pointed at Boone who was waving to get Mikey's attention again. Boone cuffed his arm and humped the air before he was yanked out the window. Mikey and Lola laughed hysterically at him. "I love them together too. Lay is a lot more serious, surprisingly. But turns into a little kid around him.

Her comment made Mikey think about what him and Layla spoke about earlier. "C'mere." He guided Lola to sit on his lap.

Lola chuckled and grabbed her cup. "Why you always tryna hold me?" She teased while on his lap.

"Cause you like when I do." He slyly remarked, making her blush as she turned away. He gently nudged her face back to his by her chin. Their gaze was intense, the world and music began to disappear as they slowly leaned in to kiss.

"Tops off lady!" A man yelled, breaking their moment. Mikey gave the man a deathly gaze. If looks could kill the man would have died in an instant. He froze for a second before apologizing and running off to his friends.

Lola and Mikey watched as his friends laughed at him for not accomplishing his goal. "Well, to us." he lifted his cup in frustration.

She lifted hers chuckling and tapped his cup. "To us," she repeated before drinking the rest of her cup.

"Let's get inside, I'll give you a tour. It's getting a little bit too reckless out here." Mikey pointed at the numerous couples that were only seconds away from intercourse in and around the pool.

Lola's eyes began to bead as she quickly got up. They both laughed as they walked into the house and Mikey noticed a guy in the distance in all black that kept looking at them. He shrugged it off thinking the man was just staring at the best-looking female at the party. He kept a mental note that someone was watching them.

They walked around the 4-story mansion viewing the rooms they could and skipping the rooms they heard people in.

"Ooooh they have a pool table," Lola said as they passed by the game room. Mikey became uneasy at the feeling of someone watching him, thinking it was the guy from before he kept his guard up. "What's wrong?" Lola asked, looking around.

"Nothing, let's get a game started." He answered, trying to act like nothing was bothering him before they started playing. Lola shrugged him off and handed him a pool stick.

"You suck," Lola said, sticking her tongue out at Mikey as she lost the tie-breaking game.

"Only says the loser." Mikey laughed. She smacked her teeth waving him off in a mocking manner. They put the sticks back and left the game room to finish looking around the house.

Mikey's uneasy feeling began to grow as they continued to walk around. He felt eyes on him from somewhere, but he couldn't find them. His gut was saying it was time to go but Lola was having a lot of fun, so he didn't want to leave just yet. They went back to the kitchen to pour themselves another cup.

Lola's smile dropped as she saw Vel outside in all black. The whole tour she also felt that someone was following and watching but she ignored it from her state of comfort and security with Mikey. Chills crawled down her spine in fear as Vel locked eyes with hers. She noticed his eyes were the same as before. She was ready to leave but couldn't leave her sister and Boone.

"What's wrong baby girl?" Mikey's voice was more stern, noticing the change in her attitude.

"Nothing, I- I think I'm just ready to go." Lola weakly chuckled, gesturing she didn't want another drink.

"You okay? We need to go to the bathroom?" Mikey pointed to the bathroom thinking she was going to throw up. She nodded telling him she was good and hid her fear and sadness from seeing Vel's face. "Okay, let's go find Bonne and Lay so we can get out of here. I think I'm ready to go too. I had my fun tonight." He said, pulling her into a hug.

"Y'all ready to go?" Boone aggressively put his arm around Mikey's shoulders. Mikey turned in frustration not knowing who touched him.

"Yo, I almost beat yo ass." Mikey jokes. They all chuckled at Mikey and Boone. Lola looked back outside seeing that Vel wasn't there anymore. She began to think that she was just seeing things but didn't want to take the chance.

"Let's get up out of here y'all," Boone said, still laughing.

Mikey looked at Lola who was nodding in agreement. "Well, let's rock." He took her hand and followed behind Boone and Layla to the car. Lola saw Vel once more and his face was even angrier. She still said nothing knowing they were about to leave.

"We gotta handle some business, but then we'll meet y'all at Lay spot later on." Mikey looked confused at what Boone had planned but shrugged it off thinking he was just going to tell him about him and Layla having sex.

"I'll see you soon baby girl," he said, hugging Lola. She nodded and headed toward the driver's side of the car only to be blocked by Layla.

"No, I'm driving, I gotta drop something off to Heather," Layla said. Mikey and Lola picked up on the weirdness of Layla and Boone. He paid it no mind thinking they had to know something, or they just had a bad time. He got in the car and waited until the girls pulled off, following behind. He honked at them when they turned off separate ways.

"Aight Boone, what we gotta do?" Mikey said as Boone continued to watch the girl's car. "Yo, everything aight?" He looked around not noticing anything.

"Y'all was getting followed at the party," Boone said watching a black car that pulled out after them turning their way. "Good" he whispered to himself.

"What?" Mikey looked back in the direction Boone was looking and saw a black car with no license plates behind them. "That's him?"

"Yeah, I saw you pick up on him, but you couldn't see where he was," Boone said, causing Mikey to pick up speed.

He took random turns to lose the black car but to also make sure they were getting followed. "Who is he?" he questioned through his mad man-like driving. He sped through side streets and back roads hoping to lose the man following them but couldn't.

"Lemme see yo gun Mike." Boone angrily smacked his teeth. He was always playful only because he was a killer at heart. He had a fire of anger that couldn't be put out unless it consumed its target. "Mikey your gun, NOW!" Boone yelled.

"UNDER MY SEAT." Mikey hastily replied, keeping his eyes on the road.

Boone quickly reached under his seat but felt nothing. "Nigga where is it?" He kept feeling around only to touch the air.

"Fuck, it probably fell to the back." Mikey realized that the car was picking up speed. The car caught up and rode beside them. The man in the car rolled down the window. "Boone your fucking gun!" Mikey yelled.

"I GAVE MINES TO THE GIRLS! WHERE IS THE GOLDEN ONE?!" Boone questioned.

"HOLD ON!" Mikey yelled seeing the man had a mask on and was holding a gun out his window. Thinking he was about to shoot, Mikey slammed the brakes and turned the wheel, hitting the back corner of the car before the shots were fired. He quickly turned the car around picking speed back up before getting hit by the back of the black car.

"NIGGA DRIVE THIS PIECE OF SHIT!" Boone yelled, finally grabbing the gun. He leaned out his window and shot at the driver in the black car as they sped off.

Mikey looked and saw the car drive away in another direction. "About time you got the gun nigga. Damn," he jokes. "I'm out here 'Midnight Club-ing' and you over there beating yah yak meat." He joked again looking out for the black car.

"Your jawn was all the way in the back," Boone exclaimed. "Where is the golden gun anyway?" He asked Mikey.

"I left it in the girl's car, I didn't wanna bring attention to myself having it if I put it back in the whip."

"Makes sense, it must've pushed this one back when you put it under your seat the first time." Boone clutched the gun tight in his hands.

"I guess so. But we need to find out who that was?" Mikey chimed.

Boone's face darkened in anger before he spoke. "It was T-YO WATCH OUT!"

Chapter 12

"It was his fault, it's all his fault. He has to die." Teivel repeatedly whispered to himself as he pulled into the parking lot. He noticed that Mikey's car was parked next to Lola's. A devilish grin stretched upon his face. His rage and hate cloud have burned a hole through his chest. He parked in a place where he could see them, but they wouldn't be able to see him. He sat in the car waiting and watching, hoping they would come out. After some time, he decided to go in and see if he could find Mikey and Lola instead. He wanted revenge, revenge on Mikey and he wanted Lola back. Teviel set it in his mind to do both. Putting his gun up knowing he couldn't get in with it on him, he fell upon some roofies. He put them in his pocket thinking of secretly drugging them both.

"Wassup T?" Metri said, patting down Teivel. "Wassup big dawg." He responded making it seem like nothing was wrong. He used to come to these parties with Boone years ago but after everything happened with Dolores, he and Boone fell out. He would catch him there frequently but never interact. "What do I gotta do to be like you when I grow up Metri?" Teivel jokes, walking past Metri.

"First step, stay out of parties like these," Metri said, waving for the next person to come up.

"But these are the best ones, everybody in here," Teivel responded.

"And that's what makes you a nobody, cause everybody is there." Metri grabbed some wristbands and put them on the females who he finished checking. "Wait, T... Here." Metri put a wristband on Teivel's arm and sent him in.

Teivel looked around the party staying within the crowd, faking as if he was dancing here and there trying to blend in the best he could. "Where are you, dammit?" He angrily whispered to himself. Walking around the mansion he went upstairs noticing Boone and Layla.

"You already know wassup Lay," Boone said as he opened the door.

Teivel secretly watched, making sure he wasn't caught. The door shut and Teivel went up to it listening to their conversation hoping to find out where Mikey and Lola were.

"Come see the balcony bae," Boone said to Layla as she followed behind. He opened the curtains showing the view of the city and the pool. "Yeah, this is my favorite room here because of the view-"

"Tiddies." Layla cut him off. Boone looked muddled until he noticed what she was talking about. "There's tiddies everywhere." They both laughed and scanned looking at all the women together.

"Welcome to choose your rack." Boone imitated a game show host as he spoke. "The beautiful and wonderful Layla, if you look here, you'll see all the different racks we have. Your job is to tell me your top three, and if you fit the criteria, you get the special prize." Boone pointed to the pool area.

"Oh, so there's a prize?" Her eyes lit up in amusement.

"All you have to do is choose the top three correctly." Boone finished. Layla rubbed her chin as she scanned the pool again.

"Her, her, aaannd her. With the huge tiddies." Boone squinted to see Layla's last pick.

"Damn, them some big ass tiddies." He broke character at the size of the woman's breast. "Those gotta hurt her back." They both laughed while scanning the pool.

"Wait what about my prize?" Layla asked. Boone gave a devilish grin that put Layla in turmoil.

"The prize is my Ph.D." He held in his laughter at Layla's face.

"You never went to school. What Ph.D. you got?" Boone's face lit up like a child on Christmas morning.

"I don't need to go to school for this Ph.D." He replied.

"So, what is it?"

"My pretty huge DIC- Look there's Mikey and Lo over there." Boone cut himself off still laughing at his joke while Layla gazed on him dumbfoundly.

"You ain't shit you know that?" She laughed before looking out the window. "I know she bet not have her tiddies out." She squinted as she looked to make sure. "Who you calling?" she asked Boone.

"You see them tiddies nigga?" He excitedly yelled over the phone.

Teivel listened to Boone's conversation, figuring out where Mikey and Lola must have been. "Outside." He whispered to himself, still listening to Boone. He didn't want Boone or Layla to mess up his plan or come looking for them. He waited patiently, hearing the balcony door shut.

"I gotta use the bathroom, I'll be right back," Layla said. Teivel hurried behind a wall making sure not to get spotted as Layla walked outside the room. He watched Layla as she went to the bathroom. He tried to get in, but the door was locked.

"There's somebody in here!" She yelled out seeing the doorknob jiggle.

"Fuck." He whispered to himself. He walked to the room where Boone was and saw him in the window doing something dumb. Deciding this was the best time to strike, he took out the roofies and quietly dropped them in the bottle that Boone had. He then crept behind Boone, who was humping the air, and yanked him out the window.

Boone was laughing until he was yanked. "Damn bae you strong as fuck." He stopped once he looked at Teivel. "Fuck wrong with you nigga?!" He angrily yelled. Boone didn't like Teivel after Dolores died; he felt like Teivel had something to do with it. His intuition was usually never wrong but he never made accusations without proof. Flames from murderous intent steamed the room from their eye contact. "I'm finna beat yo-"

"Who's this bae?" Layla walked into the room stopping the motions of Boone.

Teivel looked at Layla and smiled, her body was filled with fear at the sight of Teivel. His eyes were still black from the drugs, he looked like the devil in the eyes of Layla.

"Nobody, he was just leaving," Boone said, hiding his anger.

"I'ma see you real soon. B," Teivel said, slightly brushing into Layla's frozen body as he walked by.

"C'mere, we have to go," Boone said as Teivel left out their sight.

She nodded in agreement.

"Why is that fizzing?" She asked, looking at the bottle they were drinking. Boone walked to the bottle questioning what could have happened. He picked it up, noticing something still dissolving in it.

"You know him?" he asked.

"Yeah," Layla replied.

"How?" Boone faced Layla as she was getting back to normal after being so shaken up. She told Boone everything that happened between Teivel and Lola earlier in the day but told Boone not to say anything. He agreed not to say anything but knew they had to get out now. "When we get to the car, I'm going to give you my gun, we are going to go separate ways and meet back at your spot." he planned.

"Okay, he doesn't know where I live so that's good on our part," she commented.

"If he follows you, come to my house, if not go straight home okay," he demanded.

"Okay."

"Aight, but I'ma give you my gun just in case and here I'm finna share my location. If I don't hit you back up by 12:30 something is wrong. Find me and call the police." he is always prepared for the worst.

"I love you, Boone," Layla said.

Boone chuckled, pulling Layla closer to him by her hips. "I love you too, this won't be the last time we say this, okay," he reassured kissing her. "Let's go find them before he does." Layla agreed before they hurried to the pool.

Teivel stood in the back of the pool area watching both Mikey and Lola thinking that Boone and Layla were taken care of. He knew Boone drank when he was angry and whenever he wanted to impress a female. He knew he was in the clear and he secretly stayed in the crowd waiting until the perfect moment. He saw Mikey looking around as if he was looking for someone. Teivel turned around avoiding being seen. Mikey and Lola soon walked into the house as Teivel secretly stalked them. He wanted one of them to take a drink, but they never did so he had to wait for an opportune time. Mikey was too cautious; he didn't like the feeling of being watched and continued to scan around irritating Teviel. Teivel was almost spotted a few times so he decided to go back out to the pool to watch the kitchen, figuring they would come back to regroup before everyone left.

Fifteen minutes passed and he saw both Mikey and Lola come into the kitchen. Lola locked eyes with him. His demonized posture paralyzed her but only for a second. He waved to her, the fear in her eyes excited him. "I will have you soon." He wickedly spoke to himself, dissolving into the crowd. He took the side gate to get to the parking lot and secretly moved to his car. He waited, watching for Mikey and Lola. Mikey, Lola, Layla, and Boone all came out laughing together.

Teivel questioned why Boone and Layla were coming out. "I guess they both have to die." He said to himself, watching everyone get into their cars. His mind roared with a fury that shook his brain. His vision began to blur, and his equilibrium was spinning out of alignment from the wound on his head. He took a deep breath, pouring a handful of pills in his hand. With no hesitation, he swallowed three of them putting the rest back in the container. The high was prompt, it soothed the pain of his beating migraine before putting on a ski mask. He started up his car and followed behind another car to not seem suspicious. They left the parking lot. He saw both cars going separate ways, he thought that Mikey and Lola were in the car together and decided to follow them. He tried to stay incognito, but he noticed that the car slowly picked up speed. He contemplated on if he should keep up or try again another day but the voices that whispered in his head began to scream.

"HE TOOK EVERYTHING! KILL HIM! HE HAS TO DIE!" A demonic voice screamed in the ears of Teivel, forcing him to pick up speed to follow Mikey. They raced through back streets, drifting and sliding with every turn. He didn't want to lose this perfect chance to get his revenge. He sped up on a straight road, catching up to Mikey. Side by side with Mikey's car, he grabbed his gun and rolled down the window. Staring into the eyes of Mikey, desperately desiring to see the fear on his face but Mikey only had rage in his eyes. He screamed internally as he pulled the trigger letting gunshots off. Mikey stopped his car hitting Teviel's, forcing him to hit the brakes.

Teivel hastily put the car in reverse, speeding to hit Mikey's bumper. He bent down noticing someone lean out the passenger side window. He covered himself waiting until he didn't hear any more gunshots. Once the barrage of bullets was done, he scanned the road spotting Mikey speeding away. Teivel thought it was better not to catch up, but to catch them slipping so they wouldn't speed up. He took a couple of back streets that didn't have lights to stay unseen until he saw Mikey's car only streets away in front of him. He stomped on the gas pedal picking up speed. Anger, hate, and wrath filled his memories as the distance between the two cars forcefully closed.

"TAKE EVERYTHING FROM HIM!" The voice screamed in Teivel's mind as he insanely laughed before ramming into the side of Mikey's car.

Mikey's car flipped but landed back on its tires as Teivel's vision went black almost as if the lights were cut off. He woke up seeing nobody around but their cars. "FINALLY, I WILL KILL YOU, I FUCKING HATE YOU!' Teivel screamed as he limped to the driver's side. He peeked in seeing Boone and Mikey both unconscious covered in blood from the crash. He ran to his car wincing at the pain and tried to start it. "C'mon you piece of shit start." Slamming his fist into the dashboard as he yelled. After a couple of tries, it finally started up. He opened the doors and went back to Mikey's car, pulling out Mikey and Boone, putting them in his back seat. "Let's go on a little road trip fellas." He insanely chuckled. "I will take everything from you Mikey." he looked in the mirror to see him.

Chapter 13

Mikey awoke to a painful slap to the face. "Wake up, bitch." His vision was blurred as he finally came to. His head rang as memories flashed back in his head of the accident. "Hey, you're up. I thought I killed you trying to wake you." Teivel said with a devilish grin, he had a sinister chuckle that matched. Mikey was still in a daze from the accident. He tried to get up but was unable to move. "You can't leave yet, it's only 12:15 and the day is just getting started." Mikey squinted, finally getting his vision back, seeing Teivel standing in front of him.

"Teivel?" Teivel turned around and smiled in Mikey's face, closing the distance between them as he spoke.

"The one and only." Mikey looked over, hearing groans beside him but Teivel forcefully turned Mikey toward himself. "He's next but you're now."

Mikey's anger began to rise. "Fuck you doing T?" he questioned just to be answered with a backhand to the face.

"You only speak when your spoken too nigga." Teivel retorted. His movements were sporadic and incoherent as if he was fighting himself. "Kill him, kill him, kill him, KILL HIM!" the voices whispered and rang through his mind, echoing off the walls of his skull. "Not yet I have to take what's mine first." He confided in himself.

"What the fuck is wrong with you? When I get out of this, I'm gonna-" Mikey was interrupted by a kick to the chest. He lost his breath as his chair fell back making him hit his head on the floor.

"Now you were saying when you get out of where?" Teivel evilly jokes, sitting Mikey's chair back up. He leaned down to Mikey's face peering into his eyes eager to see the fear but was met with unrelenting anger. "Always so strong-willed. But look around, you're getting out of nothing NIGGA! I WILL BREAK YOU!" He yelled through his teeth at Mikey. In a swift motion, he grabbed Mikey by the throat lifting him slightly in the air. Mikey spat blood in Teivel's face as he gasped for air. Teivel smiled as he whipped off the spit and pulled out his gun aiming it at Mikey's head. Staring Mikey down, still wanting to see the fear in his eyes. His anger screamed in his mind while he physically laughed like a maniac.

"Take it, take it, kill him, kill him, TAKE HIS LIFE, DO IT, PULL THE TRIGGER. KILL HIM NOW!" The darkened voices in Teivel's mind screamed as he stared down the barrel of the gun. his vision began to quake, he felt himself slowly giving in to the urge to kill. He pulled the trigger, only after slightly moving the gun from Mikey's head. Mikey knew Teivel finally lost his mind.

Growing up Teivel always had something a little strange about him. He would always overdue when fighting, almost killing them, and loved to hurt people that weren't close to him. Mikey could tell that he wasn't Teivel anymore. He was the devil in flesh.

"You're fucking crazy!" Mikey yelled only to be laughed at.

"Oh yes, I know I am. But when you lose everyone and everything you love, then have the last hope ripped from your arms…" Teivel began to psychotically scratch his arm, ripping his skin as he laughed. "It's your fault!" Mikey gave a confused look. "You don't know?" Teivel put his gun down leaning into Mikey's face again before he spoke. "You took everything from me."

Mikey saw an opportunity to strike and headbutted Teivel, opening the wound on his head. "I took nothing from you!" Mikey laughed back revealing his own angered madness. Teivel froze as if the headbutt did nothing to him. Blood began to cover his face. Teivel's hand shook as he touched the blood on his head.

"You like this? How about you have one bitch." Teivel hit the butt of his gun on Mikey's head in the same place his wound was. Mikey winced at the pain. "Now just hold on to that and I'll see you in a minute," Teivel said as he left the room they were in.

"Yo Boone, get up. I need you, man." Mikey pleaded as his head spun. Boone quickly opened his eyes and looked toward the closed door.

"I woke up a little bit before he woke you up. I just acted like I was still sleeping. I'm trying to get these ropes; I almost have them." Boone whispered, never moving his position. Mikey rubbed the blood from dripping into his eye and saw the loosening of Boone's ropes. He noticed that he was handcuffed to the chair instead of tied up. Boone shushed Mikey; hearing footsteps come closer to the door.

"And the main event is back," Teivel said, bursting into the door. Teivel's wound was now partially closed, and he had a bottle of liquor and two shot glasses. "See, back then I would die to have another drink with you, but you. You never said anything." Teivel grabbed a chair and sat in front of Mikey. He poured a shot for the both of them.

"I never said what?" Mikey questioned.

"Here, take a shot," Teivel said, ignoring Mikey as he tried handing him a shot glass full of liquor. Mikey didn't even try to reach it, knowing that he couldn't due to his restraints. "Aww don't look at me like that and OPEN YOUR FUCKING MOUTH NIGGA!" Teivel yelled as he jumped up. He took Mikey's jaw and pried it open, pouring a shot down his throat. Mikey coughed as it flowed through his throat burning his chest and bubbling in his stomach.

"Okay, now where were we?" Teivel grabbed his chair, sitting it back in place. Mikey wanted Boone to hurry up but knew he had to distract Teivel before Boone made a move.

"You said I took everything, right?" Mikey said, hoping to keep Teivel's eyes on him and not Boone.

"Oh, now you want to talk," Teivel asked suspiciously, looking at Mikey who didn't respond anymore. "Well, that was fast." Teivel laughed and grabbed some pills out of his pocket. "Ahh, now that's the stuff. But my brother." Teivel stood up after swallowing a couple of them. He paced around in place crossing his arms as if he was thinking. "MY BROTHER!" Teivel screamed, throwing his chair. Teivel laughed evilly walking to Boone. "My brother is dead because of you." Teivel menacingly stared at Boone. Mikey watched as his hand trembled holding his pistol.

"Boone has nothing to do with it. I knew, just me." Mikey pleaded, wanting Teivel to come back to him and away from Boone. Teivel turned around smiling devilishly at Mikey. Fear filled Mikey's eyes at the sight of Teivel wanting to take Boone's life.

"There it is... That's what I was looking for." Teivel picked up his gun and aimed it at Boone.

"NO, STOP! I WILL FUCKING KILL YOU!" Teivel tilted his head backward-looking almost like he was possessed, his eyes were all black with a smile covering his face.

"Fear, kill, destroy, kill him, KILL HIM. KILL HIM!" The devilish voices screamed in Teivel's mind once again.

"MY BROTHER, my brother died because you didn't say anything. Gino... oh how fucked up his death was. You remember the day sweet Dolores became one with the Lord?" Mikey struggled to get out of his handcuffs at his mother's name.

"Don't you fucking say her name." Mikey spat through his teeth. The handcuffs pierced his wrists causing him to stop his movements.

"Aw, what happened? Ran out of gas?" Teivel taunts. Mikey looked into the soul of Teivel as his face was emotionless.

"I will kill you." Mikey calmly retorted.

"Kill me? NIGGA I WILL SLICE YOUR FUCKING THROAT RIGHT NOW AS WE SPEAK!" Teivel yelled. Teivel was more upset that he got frightened at the face of Mikey. All the years growing up with Mikey, he knew there was something off about him. Whenever he got that face his demeanor would change and at those moments whatever Mikey says goes. Mikey smiled evilly as he sat staring into the eyes of the devil himself. "You're one crazy piece of shit you know that?" Teivel chuckled.

Mikey didn't respond to him, just blankly stared into the soul of Teivel who didn't back down but fought the urge to kill Mikey. "You know, Gino shot my brother... right before you met me, and you said nothing? I always wondered how you got that much 'boy' and for some reason, my brother was almost killed for missing the same amount." Teivel spoke, never moving. This was a battle of wills in the face of death for both and neither backed down.

"I'm upset he didn't die the first time," Mikey said knowing he didn't mean it. Mikey loved Duke like his own big brother. Duke helped him get into the business and gave him a plan to get out and it all worked for him so far. He was also sad that Duke died, Mikey always put Duke's death on himself for not saying anything.

"I see what you're trying to do, you're tryna get in my head," Teivel said, aggressively poking his head with his gun. Mikey knew it was working but before he could continue Teivel hit him "YOU'RE NOT RUNNING ANYTHING AROUND HERE NIGGA! In here, I'm in charge!" Teivel muddled with wrath. "You're going to listen to me because you want to know what happened to poor sweet Dolores."

Mikey stayed silent, his anger and curiosity didn't allow him to speak.

"Good, don't get yourself killed too early nigga." Teivel remarked as Mikey continued to hold back his emotions. "So where was I? Oh yeah my brother, you know he died only because you didn't say anything about Gino." Teivel paced around in circles as he spoke. "Now I'm not blaming my brother's death in the beginning on you... Nah I am because if YOU WOULD HAVE SAID SOMETHING!" Teivel took a deep breath as he got control of his emotions again. "You didn't say anything, and he was 'supposedly' killed." Teivel spoke with quotation fingers. "But praise the Lord he lives, oh what a happy day. Well, for you cause your god or whatever he is you served saved another life." Teivel mocked, moving closer to Mikey leaning down to eye level.

"You know he became a Christian after that? Because of Dolores, and for what?" Teivel questioned hysterically. "The same death for the SAME DAMN REASON! Could you get that? I mean he still did everything he did before, so I guess he was still a sinner in God's eyes. That white Devil hanging on that cross don't forgive niggas like us, you know that right?"

Mikey was fuming by the disrespect to his beliefs.

"Oh, c'mon you can speak now, aren't you supposed to tell the world about your white savior Cesare Borg- I mean Je-"

"Don't disrespect my God," Mikey spoke through his teeth, cutting him off.

"Oh yeah? And tell me, will he strike me dead?" Teivel bitterly teased.

"I will." Mikey quickly retorted. Teivel jabbed Mikey in his mouth.

"Nigga what I tell you about saying you're gone kill me? Better watch yo mouth boy." Teivel laughed before collecting his composure. "So Mikey, tell me before I continue, who exactly is your God?"

Mikey didn't say a word.

"I said, what is his name? TELL ME!" Teivel grabbed Mikey's head forcefully, holding it up while looking down on him. "Aren't you spose to tell the world of his gospel? Well, WHOSE FUCKING GOD-SPELL IS IT?" Teivel screamed in a deranged manner.

"Yahshua is his name." Teivel dropped his head and punched Mikey again.

"I said god not savior dumbass."

"Yahuah," Mikey stated angrily.

"Now that you've said his name you feel more comfortable with your death?" Teivel put his gun up to Mikey's head. Boone silently struggled harder knowing his time was running out.

"Bang," Teivel whispered out loud, putting Boone at ease. He knew Boone was up after this, he noticed the small fidgeting but didn't want them to know. "Now because of your mistakes and the plan of your god or whatever Duke was killed by the same man who shot him earlier. You took something from me so I thought I should repay the favor by taking-" Teivel stopped hearing something upstairs. "We got company? I didn't invite anyone." He walked towards the door keeping in mind that Boone was free from the ropes. "Let's finish this chat. It might be my baby." Teivel turned his back to Boone who finally broke free of the ropes. Boone rushed toward him. Seeing it coming, he turned and shot.

"BOONE!" Mikey screamed. Boone held on to his chest staring into the black eyes of Teivel as he hovered over him.

"I knew you were up the whole-time nigga." Teivel said, chuckling as he kicked Boone down to the ground.

Mikey let out a roar in rage, fighting to break loose of the cuffs. "I WILL FUCKING KILL YOU NIGGA. ON MY MOM I SWEAR I WILL FUCKING KILL YOU!"

Teivel laughed menacingly as he looked at Boone who fell backward.

"Boone, get up brotha! Don't you die on me dawg!" Mikey pleaded while Teivel walked closer to him.

"I can't wait until Lola gets here… then things will really get interesting. I'm feeling a lil loose."

"HOW DO YOU KNOW HER! I WILL FUCKING KILL YOU! BOONE PLEASE… Wake up." tears fell as he fought to break out of the handcuffs.

"You know while you were fucking with Tia? MY BITCH!" Teivel punched Mikey in the face at the memory of Portia. "I fucked the shit out yo bitch. Pussy."

Mikey tried to headbutt Teivel again but missed. "I bet she kissed you after sucking my dic-" Mikey was interrupted by Teivel kicking his chest. Mikey's shoulders almost touched from the force. His chair flew back again. Teivel didn't stop, he walked over to the chair letting his anger out on Mikey through punches and kicks. Mikey tried to cover up but couldn't from the position he was in. All he could do was turn his face and lean, hoping not to get hit directly.

"You fucked my Shawty, right? Okay, let's do that." Teivel kicked Mikey once more before walking out the door. "If you touch her I will-!" Mikey was cut off by the pain and loss of breath from the barrage before letting out another lion-like roar.

Chapter 14

"Layla, what's going on, why haven't you told me anything?" Lola asked anxiously.

"Listen, at the party, Vel was there," Layla said, holding back her anger.

Lola thought she was going crazy because she saw him. "So, where's Mikey and Boone?" she was afraid now, knowing how Teivel lost it earlier that day.

"That's where we're going," Layla replied as she pulled into the dark desolate road. She drove up to a house and parked where no one would see them. "Call the police and give them our location," Layla said to Lola as she reached under her seat and grabbed the gun Boone gave her.

"Whoa! Where did you get that?" Lola was surprised that Layla had a gun.

Layla was always more serious, but Lola was the one to pull out a gun first. "We have to save them; you've seen his eyes," Layla told her. She shivered at the thought of the demon that showed itself through the eyes of Teivel.

"Is there another one under-" She reached under her seat to find a chrome pistol with gold trimmings that said 'No Remorse' engraved on the barrel. They both marveled at the beauty of the gun. "Where did this come from?" She asked. Layla shrugged her shoulders as she called the police. Lola thought back to who was in the seat last. "Mikey," she remembered. Before they went into the party he was in the seat. She smiled at his name, but it disappeared at realizing the situation he may be in.

"Aight sis, let's go," Layla said. Lola nodded and they both crept up to the house hearing yelling and screaming from inside.

"That's Mikey," Lola whispered.

"Can you hear Boone?" Layla fearfully questioned. They listened for a second hoping to hear something but couldn't.

"No...it can't be that-"

"He's with Mikey. Mikey would die before letting him die." Lola said, hiding all her worries. Layla wiped the tears off her cheeks that fell from the thought of Boone dying. She was filled with rage now wanting revenge, she tried holding on to hope but as they found a way in, she heard nothing from Boone. Only the angered roars from Mikey.

The floorboard creaked as they crept into the house. They froze in fear hoping that no one heard it. It was silent for a moment before they heard someone talking.

"Let's finish this chat. It might be my baby."

"Fuck, fuck, fuck." Layla began to nudge Lola to hurry back outside. A gunshot followed by more yelling from Mikey stopped their tracks. They both stared at each other with fear in their eyes not knowing who it was that got shot.

"Boone get up brotha! Don't you die on me dawg!" Layla's heart dropped knowing who got shot.

"Run now!" she yelled in a whisper.

"What do you mean? You come with me. We can wait until the police come, and, and, and." Lola began stuttering.

"No, you hear that. Teivel is crazy, he will find you again. I can't have that; we both know who it was that got shot. I just got to see him one more time." Lola was silent at Layla's request.

"I'm not leaving you," Lola stated hardening herself for what was coming up next. They both smiled at each other before hearing a door open. Layla pushed Lola outside, accidentally throwing her gun in the action.

"Go!" She silently yelled at Lola before hiding herself in the house. Lola hid out of view hearing footsteps coming up the last steps.

"Aww c'mon I know it's you, Lola. I miss you, baby, come give me some sugar." Teivel teased as he scanned the house. Mikey's yells filled the background. "WOULD YOU SHUT UP I'M TRYING TO DO SOMETHING," Teivel yelled, hoping that Lola would attack him in the same manner that Boone did? Layla saw his back was turned and took the opportunity to strike, being caught by a hook to the stomach. "Aww man, that works every time." He eagerly joked. He looked closer, noticing it was Layla. "Ooooh, now I see why you two are together. No wonder, you're both dumb as fuck." He grabbed Layla's hair as she clutched her stomach. She fought the pain and swung hitting Teivel in the face, she continued her barrage as Teivel dragged her by her hair.

"Now you're gone, stop putting your hands on me." Teivel pointed his gun at Layla. She stood paralyzed in fear but enraged in her heart. Teivel kicked her down the stairs he came up. "That's better" he said, following behind Layla's tumbling body. She screamed and winced in pain until the last step where she fell unconscious. "Damn. This is the reason I never liked you. You were always so loud."

Mikey watched as Layla's body fell lifelessly. "Layla!" Mikey yelled out in fear of her being dead.

"What don't you get about me taking everything from you Mikey?" Teivel said evilly. "Layla sis, please get up, GET UP, GET UP LAY PLEASE." Mikey struggled to break free as he continued to scream.

"Mmhmm not too bad," Teivel said, tilting his head to the side lustfully observing all the curves on Layla.

"You're fucking sick." Mikey spat; he was at his limit. He was tired but wrath and anger filled his mind and clouded his pain.

"I mean I already hit Lola before you did. You got you a good one." Teivel pointed to Boone as he bent down to Layla's body, seeing if she was still alive. "Oh, still alive, good. I'm not a fan of necrophilia. Creeps me out, but this will do."

Mikey twisted his wrist feeling it sprain hoping to get free. "PUT HER DOWN!" Mikey yelled. Teivel laughed evilly while he pulled his chair up, tying Layla down to it. Teivel lustfully admired the body of Layla.

"Nooo, don't do this. Leave her alone, please... I will fucking kill you." Boone whispered, reaching out to where Teivel and Layla were. Boone fought to get up but couldn't move, his body wouldn't let him from being shot. "Stop, please." Boone began crying knowing he couldn't do anything else. He tried to move but his body wouldn't let him.

Mikey began struggling, knocking the chair over hoping it would get him free, just a little bit.

Meanwhile, Lola called the police again to see where they were. "Hello? Yes please, I need help. I called earlier from Tom Avenue. How far are you guys?" Lola pleaded on the phone.

"We have our dispatchers out, they are only 10 minutes away, just hide and stay safe until we get there." Lola's anger boiled knowing the police were worthless. A scream from Layla was heard and Lola knew Teivel was up to something. "Hurry up, now. Please." Lola said sternly, hanging up the phone. Lola clutched onto the gun she found in her car, said a prayer, and walked into the house only taking a couple of steps when she heard someone else, so no one would hear any noises from her.

"I WILL FUCKING KILL YOU TEIVEL. MARK MY WORDS, I WILL KILL YOU!" Mikey screamed as Teivel caressed Layla's bare arm.

"Don't fucking touch me," Layla yelled, struggling to move. She tried her best to get up, but she was still fighting to remain conscious from the tumble.

"Please Layla, forgive me. I'm trying. Just hold on, I'll be there." Boone said pitifully crawling to Teivel.

"Oh, you're awake." Teivel laughed as the voices in his head took over, he no longer had thoughts of his own. Only desires of wrath.

Mikey struggled to try to break free, wiggling and jumping hoping, praying to just get out. His anger blinded him from the blood oozing from his wrists. He decided he needed to break the chair to get free, but he needed Teivel to pick him up.

"Aww Mikey, you gotta watch the magic show." Teivel picked Mikey up and tied a piece of dirty cloth in his mouth to stop him from screaming. "I think she needs one too, don't you think?" Teivel pointed at Layla who was also hopelessly trying to escape.

"Them boy scout knots really be working. Open your mouth." Teivel forced the cloth into her mouth. Layla screeched through her mouthguard and wiggled trying to escape. He continued hiding his intentions as he heard someone on the steps. The door behind him flung open with Lola behind it. Lola's face was filled with tears from hearing everything. Teivel swung immediately, hitting Lola making her drop to the floor.

"DON'T TOUCH HER!" Mikey spits out the cloth.

"OR WHAT NIGGA?" Teivel stepped toward Mikey, getting in his face as he spoke.

"I will kill you." Mikey spat in Teivel's face. Teivel slowly wiped off the spit in disgust before releasing his anger in punches on Mikey's face.

Lola started to wake back up as she lay there holding the gun. She noticed Teivel throwing a barrage of punches at Mikey. Lola tried to get up, but Layla vigorously shook her head for her to stay down.

"And now you." Teivel turned around at the sound of Lola getting up. He noticed the gun in her hand and rushed toward her, throwing her to the ground as she got back up. "Funny how the world goes round in circles doesn't it Gina," Teivel spoke knowing it would strike fear into her heart. Mikey had his head down, blood drooling from his mouth. "Pick your head up Mike, things are about to get interesting... Remember?"

Layla screamed through the cloth muzzle that covered her mouth. Both Lola and Layla knew what Teivel was talking about. Lola tried fighting but was easily overpowered by Teivel. He roughly grabbed both of Lola's wrists together in one hand, stretching her arms above her head. He lustfully scanned her body, licking his lips in the process.

Lola cried as she tried to break free from the pain. "LET ME GO!" She screamed. Teivel smiled and placed his hand on her bare skin. He slowly traveled his rough hand from her stomach to her breast, going under her bra. Layla continued to scream and fight until the muzzle fell from her mouth.

"Boone, Mikey, someone, please! LET HER GO!" Layla screamed, waking up Boone and Mikey who both were lifeless in movements. Teivel kissed on the neck of Lola who felt like she was going to throw up at the touch of Teivel. "You're missing the best part, Mike." He stared at Mikey waiting for him to look back as his hand slowly fell from Lola's breast to her privates. Layla cried and screamed, moving wildly, trying to escape. "You shut up, and just watch. I'm going to take everything from you, Mike. I promise," Teivel smiled evilly as Mikey finally looked up and noticed Teivel.

Chapter 15

Lola wiggled until she got a hand free and reached for Mikey's gun. Teivel saw what she was up to and hit her again, causing Mikey to scream once more. Mikey was no longer able to move his mouth or even say a word, but he screamed and roared like a starving lion at its prey. Teivel laughed as Lola fell unconscious. He then turned her around, having her face on the floor, and began to pull her pants down.

Mikey was out of options but was so blinded by rage he didn't care about his injuries. Mikey continued to twist his wrist hoping to break them, feeling the sprain get worse with every twist he made. "BOONE, GET THE FUCK UP!" Mikey screamed over the continuous cries and screams of Layla. He roared and jumped with his chair feeling it give in piece by piece. Tears began to flow as Boone never moved and Teivel finally got Lola's pants off. "Lola please wake up I'm almost there. BOONE PLEASE, I NEED YOU!" He yelled as he cried. Teivel laughed as his lustful desires caused a tunnel vision forcing him to pick up his pace.

Lola woke up feeling the cold floor stick to her skin as she was weighed down by Teivel. She immediately reached for the gun again, but Teivel pushed it away grabbing her arms and twisting them behind her back. She cried knowing she couldn't fight back. She stared into the eyes of Mikey who was in a beast-like state fighting to get free while tears and blood covered his face. She felt Teivel's rough hands on her bare bottom. Teivel ripped off her panties revealing her privates.

"No! GET OFF ME!" Lola struggled some more with her last bit of energy, Teivel was too focused on his goal to even notice. Lola and Mikey's eyes connected, freezing time in their gaze. A tear fell from Mikey who felt as if he failed everyone around him. Boone weakly grabbed Teivel's hand as it reached to pull out his member.

"The fuck?" Teivel questioned looking over to Boone who fought death himself to save Lola. "LET ME GO NIGGA!" Teivel tugged his free hand from Boone who had a death grip on him. Teivel angrily stood, holding Lola under his foot as he picked up his gun. "JUST FUCKING DIE!" Teivel yelled in frustration, shooting Boone in the head twice, silencing the room.

"Boone?" Layla sadly whispered watching the blood pour from his head. A ring filled the room as Mikey's vision turned a dark red, not from the blood but from the devilish rage that poured inside him. Mikey roared in a fury of rage. Teivel looked at Mikey in fear, watching as he got a second wind.

He jumped in the chair again, finally breaking it. He stood with the handcuffs still attached to the arms of the chair that dangled on his arm. He pulverized through the ropes on his legs tearing through layers of his shins. Mikey's tunnel vision was solely focused on killing Teivel. Teivel quickly lifted his gun at Mikey who was now sprinting toward him. Mikey bulldozed through the bullets that Teivel shot at him feeling nothing but wrath and anger. Mikey tackled Teivel, finally reaching him. "I… TOLD… YOU… I… WILL…. KILL… YOU!" Mikey screamed as he continuously punched craters in the face to Teivel. Every hit crashed like lightning on Teivel's face. Lola watched in fear, never seeing this side of Mikey whose face was blank but filled with pure darkness. Blood spewed from Teivel's face with every punch that connected.

"Mikey!" Lola yelled, hoping to calm him down. He was focused on destroying every nook and cranny of Teivel's face. Lola knew she couldn't stop him, so she untied Layla who immediately ran to Boone's lifeless body. Hugging him as Mikey continued to beat in the face of Teivel's lifeless body. Crunching could be heard from the sound of the punches that started to seep through the skull. Mikey frantically looked around, saw his golden-trimmed gun, and started to shoot every bullet in the chamber at Teivel while he screamed "Mikey..."

Boone grabbed Mikey's ankle. He stopped shooting, dropping the gun from his unrelinquishing wrath at Boone's voice. He turned toward Boone who was wrapped up in Layla's arms. He bent down and picked Boone up from Layla as she went to help Lola. Mikey held on to Boone, his breathing was scarce and began to slow down. "Fuck, fuck, fuck, don't you die on me man. You can't die on me man." Mikey cried as he rocked holding on. Boone's breathing got even slower. Boone looked into Mikey's eyes and smiled as he closed his eyes. Mike screeched in frustration wrapping his arms around Boone holding his lifeless body praying he would come back. Layla dug her face into Lola's chest letting out all her sadness.

"CALL THE FUCKING POLICE, AMBULANCE OR SUM LO. NOW! Lord don't let my brother die." Mikey prayed while tears poured from his face.

"I did, they should be here soon," Lola said shyly knowing that wasn't the answer he was looking for.

"Nigga... you look like... a bitch." Boone said slowly. He used his last bit of energy to look at Layla and smile. "I... love... you... Lay…" Boone trailed off smiling as he took his last breath. His body became limp and lifeless in Mikey's bloody arms.

Layla fell to her knees at Boone's last words. "I love you too Boone." Layla cried loudly as Lola held her. The sound of sirens filled the air as Mikey spoke. "You hear that Boone, it's the ambulance. They're gonna save you B, you gonna live. I just need you to breathe, I need you to wake up B... I need you." Mikey tightened his grip on Boone's lifeless body as the adrenaline finally wore off. Mikey winced from the enormous amounts of burning pains he felt on his chest.

"Mikey they're finally here," Lola said watching Mikey's hand drop lifelessly, blood began to pour through his shirt. "No… no… Mikey, please get up." Lola ran over and held on to Mikey's body. She was able to see all the bullet wounds that covered his body.

The sirens howled as police ran into the basement with their guns out. "Jesus Christ." The officer said putting his gun down at the sight of the girls crying and all the blood around the floor.

Chapter 16

Eight months have passed since everything happened. Mikey stood outside feeling the warm breeze past his face.

"Finally, out of the hospital, how you feeling bae?" Lola said, grabbing hold of his hand.

"It feels nice to be able to walk again," he retorted. Lola let off a small chuckle before the sound of the wind filled the emptiness of conversation. Scenes of last year floated through their minds.

"Lola, Mikey. Y'all ready?" Mikey looked over to the voice, seeing that it was Layla's. Lola walked over and rubbed Layla's baby bump as a tear slowly formed in her eyes. "Don't cry, you're gonna make me cry," Layla said, holding back her tears. "You know my emotions are everywhere with this baby." Mikey chuckled as he limped over to where they stood.

"Lil Boone, I can't wait to see you Lil man," Mikey said, looking at Layla's belly.

Layla felt the baby kick at Mikey's words. "He heard you." She said, chuckling. "Aight y'all. C'mon now." Layla playfully smacked their hands off her stomach. "I know you're ready to see the baby but we still gotta see someone first." Lola was holding onto Layla as she waddled to the car.

Mikey nodded following them to the car. The ride to their destination was quiet, no one could muster up the strength to say anything. The silence coerced Mikey to fall into a slumber as he began to dream.

Mikey held onto Dolores's hand while they walked to the doors of the rink. "You ready baby?" Dolores said, smiling at Mikey.

"Yes ma'am!" Mikey said excitedly, jumping in place. He couldn't hold in his energy, not that he was trying to.

Dolores laughed at Mikey as they continued to walk. "This is the rink…" Dolores thought to herself, watching Mikey's jaw drop at the scenery. The colored lights flickered and streamed its patterns while the music blared from the DJ booth.

"Mommy, look! Its Uncle Will and Auntie Maya!" Mikey pointed at Will and Maya who waved at them.

"Go say hi. I'm going to get our skates." Mikey screeched in happiness before running to his aunt and uncle.

"Wassup Mook," Will said, picking up Mikey.

"Wassup Uncle Will. Hi Auntie Maya." Mikey waved while Will held him. Maya walked over and kissed Mikey's cheek. Will tickled Mikey's torso with his finger and they began to wrestle in his arms until Dolores walked to them.

"You not finna keep beating up my son." Dolores joked.

"Me? He's beating me up." Will said, covering his head from Mikey's flurry of hits.

"Yeah mommy, I got Uncle Will right where I want him." Mikey laughed as he continued his playful onslaught.

"Oh, you do huh?" Will pulled Mikey off him and held him by his ankles. "Yeah, what now?"

Mikey laughed before jabbing Will in the gut, catching everyone off guard.

"That's right baby. Beat him up." Dolores said laughing.

"Yeah, get him, sweetheart." Maya also cheered.

"Since everyone is against me, I gotta kill you." Will teased poking Mikey's ticklish spots.

"I gotta pee, I gotta pee," Mikey yelled through his laughter.

"Do you really or you tryna sneak me?" Will questioned hoisting Mikey upright.

"I gotta go, for realsies." Will nodded and put him down grabbing his hand. "We'll be right back sis." Dolores nodded as they walked off.

"I like your shoes." A random boy said to Mikey, who shyly hid behind Will.

"Nah, we not doing that, c'mon... say thank you." The boy waited patiently, smiling.

"Thank you." Mikey shyly spoke.

"You're welcome."

"What do we do now?" Will asked. Mikey looked at Will as a smile stretched ear to ear before putting his hand up for a high five. The boy high-fived Mikey then high-fived Will. "That's my big dawg," Will said high fiving Mikey next. The boy walked away hearing his mom call him while Will and Mikey finished their bathroom trip.

"Are you ready to get on the floor?" Dolores asked Mikey as he ran back to the table once Will allowed him to. Mikey shook his head 'yes' intensely making them all laugh. "Well let's put on your skates." Dolores put Mikey in his skates, and everyone followed suit putting theirs on too before heading to the floor.

"You know how you slide in socks at home? Do the same thing." Dolores told Mikey. He fell a couple of times before getting the hang of the movement and balance. "There you go, baby." Dolores cheered as Mikey continued to move without help or falling. He skated on the barrier while Dolores, Will, and Maya followed behind.

"Hi again." The boy said from earlier, holding his hand in the air for a high five. Mikey smiled and jumped and gave him one. Once Mikey landed, he slipped down but was caught by the boy. They laughed as Mikey slipped a couple of times before he was able to fully stand. His mom watched and smiled at Mikey making a friend. "What's your name?" The boy asked while they skated.

"I'm Mikey."

"I'm Boone, you wanna be friends?" Mikey nodded, smiling, holding his hand up for another high five. They both jumped, high-fiving each other but slipping once they landed. They laughed as they sat on the floor tangled together.

"Hey baby, wake up." Mikey opened his eyes to the soothing voice of Lola. "We're here." He wiped the tears that fell from his eyes as he looked around. They got out of the car and walked to their destination, in silence. No one was able to spark up a conversation.

"This is a nice spot sis," Mikey said, closing his eyes as he let the warm breeze glide across his face.

"I tried to pick the best spot for him," Layla said waddling behind Mikey with Lola's help.

He smiled at her walk as they caught up. "I promise brotha." Mikey held onto Layla and Lola in a loving embrace. He looked at the Tombstone of Boone before letting a tear out as he continued to speak. "I know you hear me... I'm going to take care of them." Mikey said, looking into the sky letting his tears fall, hoping that Boone could hear him.

Acknowledgments

This book is dedicated to my family. They pushed me to always be better than who I am today and to ALWAYS stay true to myself. God made us all in a specific way, he made us special even if you don't see it on the outside… It's roaring on the inside. The real you. You just have to let it out.

Peace I leave with you, *my peace I give unto you: not as the world giveth, give I unto you. Let not your heart be troubled, neither let it be afraid.*
~Yahshua Hamashiach~
John 14:27

Instagram: @Mikeylotheweirdo

Email: Mikeylotheweirdo@gmail.com

Made in the USA
Middletown, DE
14 September 2022

73362216R00056